When the Rain Comes

...provides a strong emotional impact.
Tangent Online

Tumbling Dice

Good Gonzo kind of a tale.
SF Revue

Companion

...recommended reading.
Tangent Online

Daily Teds

*...I'm reminded of The Sorcerer's Apprentice, if those brooms
had really gotten out of hand.*
Locus

After

A beautiful piece of microfiction, exquisitely crafted.
Tangent Online

I Dreamed You Were a Spaceship

Nicely told lyrical tale.
SF Revue

Define The Color Blue

Chilling.
SF Revue

Home for Christmas

...a lovely piece, even more impressive for all it manages to accomplish at a relatively short length.

Locus

The Odds

May the worst side win, as usual.

Locus

The Blue Lady of Entanglement Chamber 1

Good solid story.

SF Revue

Kagari

Perhaps there is a root of a brighter tomorrow in this sad soil.

SKJAM! Reviews

Often and Silently They Come

...it is the Carrisi that are truly aline. Interesting.

SFRevue

Hillman, Charles Dallas, Ag:35. No Partner. Parents: Deceased

...There's an appeal and gravitas to stories that start out in a okey vein and gradually gain depth and pathos as they progress.

Tangent Online

1101

Digital Stories in an Analog World

RON COLLINS

SKYFOX
PUBLISHING
Science Fiction

Skyfox Publishing
353 E. Bonneville Ave
Las Vegas, NV 89101

ISBN-10: 1-946176-99-0 (Trade Paperback)
ISBN-13: 978-1-946176-99-8 (Trade Paperback)
ISBN-13: 979-8-90107-000-0 (Hardcover)
ISBN-13: 979-8-90107-001-7 (Digital)

Table of Contents

For the rivet heads.

You know who you are.

Foreword

Some time ago I published *1100 Digital Stories in an Analog World*, which included, naturally, the first dozen of my stories that saw initial publication in *Analog Science Fiction and Fact* magazine. It was a lot of fun and has proven to be popular enough that I'm even more excited about this volume, which of course is its companion—comprised of the next thirteen stories (or, as my geeky friends immediately grasp, 1101) that found homes in that historical publication. A science fictional baker's dozen, as it were.

Comparing the two volumes is interesting because they are all me, but together, the two document how my writing has grown and changed over time. Thematically and structurally, these thirteen stories feel more adventurous. Not deeper, exactly, but maybe I'm, at times, more vulnerable. Stories like "Tumbling Dice," and "Companion" are more exploratory than the tales that showed up in *1100*. "Kagari" and "The Blue Lady of Entanglement Chamber 1" are efforts to convolute genre, as is "Companion," for that matter.

Those make me particularly happy because they stand as testimony to my idea that the main thing that matters for a writer is not genre or tropes or anything else, but that one really does have to be *interesting*. All three of those are interesting stories.

As I'll note in its afterword, "Home for Christmas" is a companion piece to "Deca-Dad," but where "Deca-Dad" is lighthearted and optimistic about the concept of wanderlust, "Home" touches on the darker side of it.

I'm not sure I could even have written "When the Rain Comes" earlier in my career.

And then there's "After," which holds a special place in my heart for reasons I'll get into when the time comes.

The stories in *1100 Digital Stories in an Analog World* are, on the whole, more upbeat, dare I say optimistic in their sometimes darkish worlds. *1101* isn't exactly dour, but the stories here feel broader to me.

In the foreword to the first volume, I wrote that it was fair to say that the *Analog Science Fiction and Fact* magazine holds a special place in my heart. Duh, right? *Analog* and its sibling publication *Asimov's* were top-tier magazines. And *Analog* in particular held much prestige, having come from *Astounding* (essentially the first-ever SF magazine, which began printing almost a century ago, now).

That's why it's a blast to look at these two volumes and realize I was able to make a contribution to the publication.

Twenty-five stories in all. Thirteen of them here.

I do so love them all.

I hope you do, too.

Ron Collins
Las Vegas, NV

Tumbling Dice

ANALOG JULY/AUGUST 2015

Side One

Jupiter Kelly, better known to most as "Jupe," was the shooter when the love of his life stepped onto the smoke-filled floor of the Starshine casino (the Starshine being the most notorious of the casinos in the Nellcote Resort, a station in geosynchronous orbit around Artoga, the fourth planet of the Luytens system).

He felt her even though she came in at his back.

There was this link between them, pure and simple.

She breathed and he exhaled. She moved, and he felt the heat. It was like they talked without their mouths ever moving. Like they fit.

He got these things sometimes, you know? Sensations. Hunches. Numbers that crystallized clear as deep space. Never about a woman, though. Before Kaatji came into the Starshine, Jupe always figured the universe held two kinds of women—ones who played the games, and ones who played the players. He respected the hell outta the first, and tried to get the hell outta the way of the second.

So, when he felt her that night, his first thought was: *How is it, after all this time, after all the dives, and after the all-too-few nights in penthouse suites, after bars and hookups in the weirdest damned nooks in the universe, after gambling with Garredine in the Oort cloud, and running with the Passi gang on Vega three, after almost hitching my wagon to that firebrand in the Draconis asteroid belt, after all this, how is it that I'm just getting to know there's a third kind of woman?*

The idea almost froze him.

Almost brought him to his skinny-assed knees, because while Jupe Kelly was actually a *good* man at heart, he most definitely was also a skinny-assed man, a man of few needs who was used to sleeping anywhere he might need to, and used to getting out of town in ways he hadn't planned. He was also a man the Galactic Gaming Commission had put on their "Last Play" list, which meant that—as he had been so kindly informed by three Mendaash security flunkies—his money was welcome, but if he was ever caught doing anything strange on the floor again he would be summarily put out of pretty much everyone's misery.

The GGC cares about guys like Jupe Kelly because guys like Jupe Kelly come into places like this carrying baggage no one can see. They care because they've got their reputation to uphold. Just like other folks care, too, like others with big reputations and bigger bankrolls than a weak asteroid like Jupe Kelly could ever manage to come upon all by his lonesome.

Turned out, being a Lister was fine by Jupe because it served to add a grain of risk to the mere act of walking onto a floor, which was like honey to his bee. It was the kind of danger that got his buzz on.

She crossed the room and stood next to him like he knew she would, the smell of her drink all lime and tonic. She was slim, and slinkly like Vegans get when they grow up on a planet with a bit lower gravity than most. Her skin was tinged to the red side of purple at the shoulders and to the blue side as his gaze slid down her arms. She wore bangles that revolved around her like planets and shined light on her from every angle.

"What's your name, baby?" he said, barely able to get the wind out.

"Kaatji," she said.

And the moment the waves of her voice pushed against his sensitive eardrums was the moment Jupe knew beyond any doubt that there wasn't a damn thing that could touch the two of them when they were together. They were a binary pair, atomic particles connected by forces strong and weak and strange and charm, they were stronger than nature herself, they were the dream and the dreamer.

It was as much truth as Jupe needed.

And those dice, they burned in his hand.

He kissed her then. It was a kiss he would be drowned for, a kiss that would make him mutiny, a kiss that said she would be the death of him. But he didn't care. That's the thing about men like Jupe and their dreams. It's the chase that does it. The dreams happen or they don't, but men like Jupe don't care because it's the chase that matters.

So he kissed her, and he rolled the dice, and they came up his point on a pair of threes that paid off for two guys playing their six-the-hard-way bets, and then he was off on a run like he had never been on a run before, on a tear, a jag of monumental proportions. People were cheering and clapping, and Kaatji, she was sayin' he needed to "kiss me quick" before every throw, and he was blazing a trail as hot as a fucking M-Class star gone nova.

And the money. Ah, the money. Thousands of Galactic Gigs rolled in, red chips and green, blue chips and black. It coulda been X-Ray cash, as far as Jupe cared, though. Could been infrared. Micro-effing-wave. It was all invisible to him.

Meant nothing.

He had done the other thing before, you see. He once had the wife and the car and the house with a view of twin moons. He once had the steady job that paid whether he did anything or not, paid enough to breathe, anyway—enough to make him need to come back for more, but not enough he could actually live. Sucked his soul, he said some nights after he had too much scotch and not enough water, sucked it drier than a desert.

He saw Kaatji's tell a mile away, of course.

You can't be around as long as Jupe Kelly had and still miss the way her eyes slid past the dark-skinned woman who came to the other side of the table dressed in black as dark as her skin and trying so hard to be ignored. Deuces were wild, he thought, and when the Lady in Black started laying bets right with him, then started playing more odds behind those bets ... well ...

He'd been rolled a time or two before.

Fool me once, baby, and it's on me. He wasn't planning on being fooled twice.

And the full truth was that even *before* the Lady in Black came to the table, Jupe had felt Kaatji change the dice out. It happened during that first kiss. He couldn't for the life of him figure out how she pulled that trick off, but it happened right there in his hand, and all he could say was that he felt it in the dice themselves. Something subtle, something deep, maybe something fucking sub-atomic—he wasn't a goddamned nuclear physicist, though, so how the hell would he know? But facts are facts, and the facts were that she pulled a move that was slick as ultra-fine oil, and those bones were different now.

Will they play? his eyes asked the first time Kaatji wrapped her pearlescent fingertips around his hand and blew her minted breath over his knuckles. *Will they pass scans from the pit bosses and the composite monitors and the base weight checks programmed into the very tables themselves?*

Jupe knew about the sensors, after all, and the sensors knew about him.

Her eyes sparkled, telling him she didn't *know* the answer. Not for sure, anyway. They said Kaatji was here to find out.

Didn't matter, though.

Because the adrenaline in that gaze was like sex amplified by a billion. It was an electric bolt mainlined down his spine, the most kick-assed, quantum-constant icing on the cake. Ever.

She kissed his knuckles, and his knees nearly buckled. The sharp edges of the dice bit into his palms. Only one way to live, he thought as he watched the dice tumble.

Only way to fucking live.

Side Two

Kaatji's plan called for the man to be just another deadbeat from some distant world, here to get blasted and complain about the river of money that kept running through his hands.

But this man didn't feel like a deadbeat.

He was tired, sure. He had seen better days. His shirt was untucked, his collar torn and frayed at the edges. He was a man who had lost everything, probably more than once, but there was still something inside.

He had, for example, *known* she switched the dice.

Maybe it was the time shift, maybe it was the scrub from the stasis field she flipped before the swap. It didn't really matter how he had done it, though, what got her attention was the fact that he had done it so easily, so naturally, and that he had done it with barely any reaction at all. The man kissed her like nothing she had ever felt before, too, and he threw the dice even though he knew *something* was different about them.

She liked the way his eye glittered. She liked how his lip curled before he threw the bones, how he opened his hand to let her blow into them, and how he grinned as her breath turned into the whistle she was using to change the program. She liked how he rattled the dice, she imagined herself as one of them, rolling around inside his hand, her carbon juggling its internal coherence, altering its center of gravity to bring up the numbers her program called for.

So, yes. He had her interested.

But Kaatji couldn't lie to herself. She knew the look of instant attraction in Jupiter Kelly's eyes. It happened everywhere she went. It happened with the Kendarian jumper driver, happened with the humans in the jumper cabin. Just as it had happened with Delvari. She couldn't stop it. She couldn't help being coveted, couldn't help being adored. It just happened. And in the end, she found the "always on" switch was at least as lonely as the "always off" switch.

Why are you here? she would think as she stared into yet another set of admiring eyes. *Why should I trust you? Why, of all the people in all the worlds, should I think you are the one who loves me for who I am rather than simply because my quantum perfume has given you a constant emotional hard-on?*

Fuck it.

That's why she waded through life alone. And that's why she played the wild girl, why she left men and women (and the occasional other) in her wake like so many used socks. Sure, the wild-girl thing could be fun at times, but it was hard to maintain. She did it because, while everyone loves a crazy girl for a night, doing something outlandish, doing something crazy-stupid every day, well, it let the clingers—the sloppy-tongued puppies who stuck by her side like addicts, but who were so clueless about who she really was—it let them see her slinking away as pre-ordained. It kept them from missing her, kept them from thinking the problem was theirs— which was all for the best.

She still remembered Leila, poor dead Leila, who had been the last to overdose on her.

She couldn't stand for that to happen again.

It was lonely life, though, this wild-girl thing.

That's why she was here, after all.

She was going to change herself, was going to fix things, she was going to find something in the very molecular structure of her being she could tweak to make her stop releasing this wavefront of pheromones, or to stop creating this electric field from her nervous system, or whatever other thing the doctors said might be firing her constant come-hither beacon.

She was so close.

Her black-market lab was able to adjust molecules now. She could change the physical properties of things with a pre-programmed command. That's how she was adjusting the dice rolls, of course. With some more lab time, she might be able to turn this thing inside her off. With maybe just a few million more Gigs, she might be able to be normal.

But she was flat-out busted now.

So if you get the idea that Kaatji was at the Starshine that night because she needed the money, you're figuring it right. And if you're thinking she knew in advance she would need help to pull it off, you are once again on the right path.

So she took Delvari in. Delvari, who was a programmer Kaatji was working with, Delvari, who knew what she was doing, and who was young and beautiful and impressionable. Kaatji hadn't had a friend for a long time, and Del had been so sweet, and sincere in her approach that for a while Kaatji had convinced herself that Del actually wanted the real her. She knew better now, of course. Delvari was a scientist at heart, more interested in the mechanics of realtime material management than anything Kaatji brought to the table.

It was fun while it had lasted, but the truth hurt Kaatji as much as their eventual separation would gnaw at Del.

She was thinking about that when Delvari stepped up to the table, just like they had planned.

* * *

Jupe had seen their game before, inside out, enough to make you sad. He could tell it was a game by the way Kaatji and her girlfriend ignored each other.

He should probably be mad.

Should probably have just put her off to the side and focused on the game.

Screw it. Kaatji was different. Kaatji was overwhelmingly, smotheringly *different* from every other woman he had ever known.

He wondered about their game. What were they doing? How were they doing it? The Lady in Black carried calmness about her like it was a blanket. She moved with stealth, made bets in silence, occasionally slipping in an odds wager. She did not drink, and she smiled with something Jupe took to be irony as she raked in her money.

Yes, the Lady in Black was behind it all.

She was also In The Way.

He came to this conclusion over a period of two hours—roll after roll, after roll, after roll. The table was buzzing by then, and it was buzzing even harder when the run was still alive another hour later. By that time, Jupe was getting uncomfortable with the stares from the pit boss. He knew it was all coming to an end, though, when he hit his point eight, and, rather than keep playing, the woman in black picked up her chips and stepped away.

Four rolls later—after just over three standard hours, and one-point-two million Gigs—Jupe Kelly crapped a yo-leven coming out, and it was over.

He received a standing ovation and a Cassiopeia Mai-Tai toast. "I'll meet you in the bar, baby," he told Kaatji as he went to the cashier's counter.

"I'll be there."

He knew she would be, too. The 1.2 MegaGigs he was going to be carrying around didn't hurt, but mostly he knew she would be there because they were destined to fly together. No doubt in his mind.

Then he received the visit he had been expecting from the moment he first rolled Kaatji's dice.

They took him to the back room.

"Mr. Kelly," Yanton Xe Den, the casino manager, said from behind his desk. "Please sit down."

They proceeded to have a discussion about odds and runs, and the impact that cheating might have on Jupe Kelly's long-term health, during which Xe Den proved to be quite comfortable with the use of threats. He also proved to be adroit with numbers and history, informing Jupe that only fifteen such runs were on record books at casinos around the galaxy. But the most important thing Jupe learned was that Xe Den was upset because no one could finger him as a cheat because they couldn't figure out how Jupe Kelly had done it.

"You know what will happen if we discover anything," Xe Den said.

"I just rolled the damned dice," Jupe replied.

After nearly forty-five minutes, Mr. Xe Den received a full analysis of the dice he had used as well as a high-level briefing of the scanning systems reports, and finally kowtowed to the idea that, yes, Jupe's winnings were legit.

"Where would you like your money?" he asked.

"Certified voucher."

"I'll have the draft prepared."

"Any chance I could take the dice? Sentimental value, you know?"

"I don't think that would be wise."

"It would speak well of the Starshine. Good for the public image, right?"

Xe Den sighed. "I'll have them sent to you."

Jupe stood to leave, then paused to set his hook.

"You might take a look at the lady in black who was at my table, though."

"And why might we do that?" Xe Den was obviously interested.

"Saw her playing cards afterward."

"And that would be a problem because?"

Jupe smiled, and shrugged. "Just sayin'," he said, stepping away, and knowing what happened to people a Lister suggested might be cheating. That's what you get when you play with the big boys, though.

He picked up the voucher at the cashier's counter, the found Kaatji at the bar and waved the key to the penthouse at her.

"Wanna see the stars?" he said with a smile.

* * *

Kaatji was anxious as she mixed a pair of drinks. She liked Jupe, but she wanted the money. No, she thought, one-point-two million Gigs bought a lot of research. She *had to have* the money.

The suite was beyond impressive, though. It was set into the shell of the station and had walls that rounded upward like a bowl. Its ceiling was a dome made of crystal that made the room feet like being in a clam shell in one way, but it also made her feel small, as if she had a front-row seat to viewing the galaxy, which, Kaatji figured was probably true enough.

"Come here," Jupe said.

She turned, handing him his glass.

He put it on the edge of a wheel of fortune sitting on the low table beside the net screen, then motioned her to put hers on the opposite side. Once both were stable, he spun the wheel slowly, watching her reaction as he did so. She saw his lack of trust in that gaze, she saw he was testing her to see if she had dropped something in his drink. Not that she could blame him. In fact, seeing his guard go up made her assess him differently. She liked it, or at least she *wanted* to like it. It meant he was fighting her, didn't it? It meant he could control his body.

Or, was she just clutching straws? Did she want someone to be interested in her for anything beyond the obvious so badly that she was seeing patterns that didn't exist?

Stop it, she told herself. *Keep your mind on the job.*

Jupe stood up and arched his back, looking out into the stars. He put his arm around her waist, and turned her so neither of them could follow the glasses as they spun down.

He motioned to the stars.

"Where have you been?" he asked.

"Nowhere, really."

He smiled, then spent considerable time pointing out star systems he had been to. His stories flowed together. They were gritty stories, mostly, drinking stories and gambling stories, and stories about chases and short-time jobs. But she liked the tone of his voice, and she liked when he spoke about caverns on one planet and a river full of red algae on another. When he was done, picked up both glasses, and handed her one.

"Time to play another game?"

The liquid burned her throat.

"You planning to tell me about the dice any time soon?" he asked.

For a moment she thought that maybe she *should* tell him. She *wanted* to tell him, wanted to trust him. But that was insane. She hadn't even known Jupe for a full day, and none of those stories screamed "trustworthy."

She kissed him, then.

Jupe thought it was in the drink, of course. But the drug was in her saliva, it was in her touch. She kissed him as much to keep him from talking as to administer the dose. It hurt her to think of him waking up alone and broke, like a million other men had done over the history of space and time, but she knew the score going in.

He laid her back on the bed and they did their thing.

As they finished, her thoughts rubbed against him like they were another part of her body. He smelled like sand and reminded her of the beach on Carraway Island, lean and raw. Then she was standing and staring up into the stars, and thinking about the world, thinking about opportunity and dreams and a lack of limitations that seemed suddenly not so impossible. She wobbled, though. The drink had been strong, and she hadn't eaten anything for a long time.

"Looks like you got the lucky number, baby," Jupe said with a shit-eating smile she could hear more than see.

"I didn't put anything in the drinks."

"It's all right, baby," he said, sitting up. "I see you got something going on. I won't hold nothing against you before you get to know me."

He put his hands behind his head, and his eyes closed slowly. His words sounded like his tongue was made of rubber. The drug was coming on.

"I don't know what you girls did with the dice, honey. But it wouldn't have mattered. We wouldda won anyway."

His voice was fading, but his words played on her mind.

I see you got something going on. We wouldda won anyway.

It sounded silly, but Kaatji knew he meant it. If only it were all true. If only he actually understood what he was saying.

"But ... shit," Jupe said. "I'm jush shhhow happy to find ya now, baby. Jush shhoow happy ... we're gonna be great ... sweetie. You'll see."

The right side of his face stopped moving, and the truth dawned in his eyes.

"Whadda hell?"

"I'm sorry," Kaatji said as he faded away. And, if she were speaking openly here, she would tell us how troubled she was to discover she actually meant it.

It's just better this way, though, she thought as she gathered up her clothes and the few other things she needed, and she gave Jupe Kelly one more glance before she slipped out of the room. *It's just better this way.*

Side Three

Jupe Kelly had never *needed* much of anything before—never taken much from anyone, never really cared about making anyone else happy. But he needed Kaatji. He needed her touch, needed her senses wrapped around him like her legs had been wrapped around him the night before. Yes, that's right. For the first time in his life, Jupiter Kelly actually wanted something, wanted *someone* badly enough he was willing fight the very tides of the world for them.

So, when he woke up and found the money was gone, it didn't bother him much—he never could keep a Gig much past moonset, after all.

But when he woke up feeling like a hot poker had been jammed into his heart, and with his head pounding like it was being hit with an effing sledge hammer, and with every cell in his body feeling like it was effing ready to effing explode and thinking that if this effing explosion happened he just hoped he would leave an effing rain of molecular goo on the entirety of the spacescape above him, well ...

That fucking hurt.

He screamed in the dark.

He ripped the sheets, and he crashed the table, and he sent the wheel of fortune spinning madly across the room. He threw bottles. He turned over nightstands, and he kicked the bed hard enough he probably broke his toe.

This called for Drastic Action. It called for the bigest, most dangerous bomb in the most over-stocked arsenal in the universe.

He didn't care if he got toasted for it. Didn't care if he fried. Screw it if it blew up in his face. The lady in black, he thought, panting like a beast—this woman from the Vega system who had set the whole thing up—she was going down. Then Kaatji would be free.

The only arsenal a man like him builds, though, is the truth and a set of connections a parsec long, and even though it felt like he was holding the butt end of a 90 gauge Gamma Gun, he hooked to the Q-net, and he dialed up the biggest motherfucking blaster he had, pulled on a connection so bold and audacious he nearly wet his own pants just thinking about it.

"Hogie, buddie," he said to the chief snitch of the Passi family, the meanest, baddest crime gang in the entire Vega system. "I got a line you need to hear, man."

"What's it on?"

"A woman cheating a casino to the tune of maybe two MegaGigs."

The connection got quiet.

"You there, Hogie?"

"Shoot," the man finally said with enough greed on his voice that Jupe could see him wiping his grimy sleeve against his drooling little chin.

It was an ugly enough image that he might have been repulsed if it wasn't for the fact that a moment later he was staring at a star he had pointed out to Kaatji, and remembering the way her heartbeat rose as he described it.

Kaatji. Kaatji. Kaatji.

The name rolled around in his head.

I'm making odds, baby, and I'm laying my last bet on you.

Side Four

The Passi family picked Delvari Kash-al up at the jump station, and they took her back to their haunts in Vega. Rumor has it that they pulled this and that out of her, but still could never find much about anything past the 800 KGigs she had cashed out, which, if you did the accounting like the Passis did left about 1.2 MegaGigs unaccounted for.

They cared, you see, the Passis, they cared about the reputation of their region. They made their living by knowing what goes down in their sector, and when an atomic engineer from their home turf goes rogue, well.

Let's just say losing the money wasn't the biggest of Delvari Kash-al's problems.

But this isn't Delvari's story.

* * *

So we pick it up with the image of Kaatji walking in the desert. The morning gave way to midafternoon, and it grew hot inside the station. It was dry enough that her feet kicked up a rough cloud of red dust as she walked through the Desert Romp, a touristy area full of fake cactus and pre-fabbed lizards that was built to attract the family types. She was headed back to the hotel, tired and limping with the results of an ankle she was stupid enough to turn as she ducked out on Delvari.

Vendors called to her as she walked, just as vendors did every time she walked any street in public. "Come on, baby," they said. "Come on over here." She felt the heat of their stares. A woman came to Kaatji and ran a finger down the side of her face. She jerked away and kept walking.

It was draining, you know, so draining to be always on.

And she felt the weight of the voucher, too, that 1.2 MegaGigs tucked down in her brassiere strap like it might be just a simple grocery slip. So she walked with her limp weighing down one side of her, and the voucher like a block of cement weighing down the other.

She had a conscience, too, of course.

She didn't want any of this.

Leaving Del to the Passis hurt her in more ways than she wanted to admit. But she was past the point where self-sacrifice was ever going to be her way. She was a survivor. She'd come too far to give any quarter now.

The sound of a jumper came down the line as if it might be drawing up next to her. It's a low sound, like a rock rubbin' on down to her soul. Hundred-to-one it was Jupiter Kelly because, you know, when it rains it pours.

Sure enough.

* * *

Jupe turned the jumper around and rode slowly beside her. She limped farther.

"Hot, i'n't?" he said.

"I can make it."

He pulled the dice out of his pocket, realizing then that everything about life is about chance. Everything. Even the old times before he went to the street. It was pure chance he met Moll back then, and the act of getting married and settling down was chance that followed that. What if she'd said no, after all? She could have. And it was chance that he couldn't hack that life, and (for the first time ever) he wondered what the odds were that Moll would have decided to join him on the road if he had actually had the decency to ask. Slim. Certainly slim, but not zero. Who the fuck knew what woulda happened then, eh?

Chance.

It was all chance that brought him and Kaatji to this very place at this very time.

He held the dice up again, propped between his fingers.

Kaatji came to a stop.

"You broke my heart, darling," he said.

"Sorry about that."

"I'm over it now."

"Well, that's a first."

He stared at her. "I can't get a line on you, Kaatji. I mean, I'm thinking about you and that other girl and the dice, and I don't see the angle."

"I don't have an angle."

"Now you're just flat-out lying."

While she remained silent, Jupe considered his own lie.

He *had* figured an angle—the dice themselves. He just couldn't see what she had done to them, and why. But he had seen the expression on her face as she looked into the stars, and he understood that the veneer of casualness she wore like a badge of courage was just that—a veneer. She wasn't the wild woman she put on. She lived with risk, but she accepted it like a sentence rather than owned it as a dream. Inside that veneer Kaatji was a woman who wanted something bigger out of life, and he wanted to know what it was.

"I can help you," he said.

She pulled her hair away from her eyes.

"No, Jupe. You can't."

"Willin' to try."

"Wish I could know that was true," she said.

"Maybe just we let your dice decide."

He opened his hand, showing her the dice Xe Den had delivered to his room just before he checked out.

"What's the game?"

"Over/under seven. I win, we run together for a bit, just to see."

"What about the money?"

"It's best we burn that either way. And it's probably best we get about as far away from Vega as possible. Sorry about that."

She sighed, and squinted against the fake sun. She figured that's what was going to happen. The money was gone, and staying out of the way of the Passi clan meant she wasn't going to be able to keep working with her current group of black-list scientists in the home system. Maybe she could convince a few to move worlds.

Maybe.

Jupe leaned closer to her. "This isn't really about the money, is it?"

The pain in her eyes went deeper than he wanted to admit seeing. She chewed her lip, and seemed to come to a conclusion.

"I roll. You call," she said.

Jupe dropped the dice into her hand, feeling the heat of their closeness, but not touching her. He wasn't sure he could handle it if they touched.

"What do you call?" she asked.

"Over."

Anything over a seven and he was a winner. Under, and he was alone again. But he knew one thing for certain now—this roll of the dice was not going to land by chance. He had seen Kaatji's mind turning, saw her making decisions, saw her run her eyes up and down his face as she talked to him.

He knew Kaatji could call the number.

But he thought that maybe, Kaatji just needed an out, a way to fool herself into letting him stay, or at least a way to let him *think* she hadn't decided to connect to him all by herself. A way to remain aloof and unconnected, yet still *be* connected.

So he waited while she shook the dice.

* * *

The dice were sharp in her hand, and the weight of Jupe's gaze was heavy as the heat. When she agreed to the wager, she had every intention of rolling her six and being done with it. A clean cut heals best.

But, the moment she shook the dice, these thoughts went through her brain:

Screw her body chemistry, what if she had actually found someone who would give up everything for her? He was a good man, or at least an interesting one. What if she actually deserved someone now?

And, in another part of her brain she thought:

How was this fair to him? With him drawn to her by his base instinct, with his body chemistry floating on hers like a lifeboat in a storm?

And finally, she thought:

What would happen when she found the answer, what would happen if she got herself good and fixed? Would Jupiter Kelly still want to be with her?

And, yes, that entire thought went through her brain in that one split second because this is the kind of brain she had.

It would be so easy.

Roll less than seven she was free and clean. All she needed to do was execute the series of whistles that would set the program.

She looked at Jupe, sitting in his jumper.

She wanted so much to trust him.

Maybe that was a truth about life or love. Maybe you never know anything, maybe you just decide to trust, and only later find out what's real.

Kaatji threw the dice, then.

Without blowing on them, without whistling, without setting a program, Kaatji threw the dice across the jumper's cowling.

* * *

The dice clattered against the wind screen as if it was the wall of a table.

The numbers blazed in the sun.

Jupe grinned. Kaatji lowered her gaze for a moment, then looked out where the horizon should be.

It was a pair of fives.

Ten.

The hard way.

Ron's Afterword

At first publication, the *Tangent Online* reviewer said this: *"Tumbling Dice" combines a casino heist (complete with confederates and betrayals), a love story, and a dream about normalcy, with themes of fate and addiction. An inveterate gambler and a genetically aberrant femme fatale who can't turn off her come-hither collide at a craps table, each playing a different game.*

I like that.

This *is* a love story, isn't it? A romance of a sort, I guess, though if one tried to categorize it under romance genre tropes, you'd probably have to call it a Meet Not So Cute. So, I guess nix going that far with the romance idea.

I sat down to write it in response to a call for an anthology themed around risk-taking. Alas, it wasn't what that editor was looking for, though I (being biased) thought it fit just fine! This story is 100% about risk in every way. Two broken people, or three, depending on how you look at it, who run into each other inside a broken world, all of them working against high odds on a moment-by-moment basis, with plans that likely will not succeed, but dreams that make it impossible to stop.

I loved writing these characters, and of course, was thrilled when *Analog* chose to put it in their pages.

The writing itself was quite visceral to me, too, because I wrote it while mainlining the Rolling Stones' *Exile on Main St*. This is at the root of why I chose the conceit of breaking the story into four sides (rather than four chapters), and of course this is the root of the story's title—which made total sense in all ways, then.

Indeed, in my mind I call the story my retelling of that album, simply because I had fun letting the music directly influence the work I was doing.

Often and Silently We Come
ANALOG JULY/AUGUST 2017

The electrons at the leading edge of X-jin's essence linked into the fine control sequence of the body probe. The student followed behind, positrons flaring in the media. 58-9 was the latest in the never ending series of cherts X-jin had been assigned to mentor. It would not be the last.

The research pod had been on the planet for half its rotation, and the exploratory drones had finally acquired the sample that was now splayed out and constrained atop the chamber's examination slab. They had work to do.

"It's *asleep*," the student sent as it connected to the sensor feed and made its first pass at the sample stream.

If the student was going to learn, the flaw had to be corrected when it first appeared. So despite their distinct lack of anti-space X-jin responded on the first available pulse.

"We are scientists," X-jin said. "That means we use precise language. Unlike us, this creature is gendered as a traditional male. Hence *he* is a *he*, not an *it*."

"I acknowledge, Master X-jin. I apologize for use of the neutral."

"Accepted. And, yes, we have him under sedation."

"I wish we could examine him in his conscious state."

X-jin waited for three pulses before replying. All students were bothersome, but 58-9 was becoming more annoying than most.

"Chemical beings have no capacity for disassociation," X-jin finally responded, "so they react poorly if they are not taken down. This means that examining a sample while it retains consciousness is difficult in the best of situations. In addition to that, our currently assigned Fold will reach the crossover junction before this cycle of darkness is completed, so we have no anti-space available for dealing with either such struggles *or* such useless communications. Please provide your focus so we are not forced to take another sample."

"Understood," the student said.

Not that it would matter.

X-jin had been through this before.

The probability of finding the answers they sought in this sample were as close to non-existent as mathematics could get. The combination of 58-9's youthful excitement and its incessant questioning had made X-jin's emotions bleed through the laminate to the point that it took several pulses to gather them back.

X-jin turned to the creature on the slab.

It was a Pakesshi, large even for a male.

Its body spanned the entirety of the open space, and was segmented into three components, each covered by a chitinous exoskeleton that varied in spectrum from black at the joints to multi-hued blues at the broader spans. The arms and legs were lanky and were used by the Pakesshi to leap great distances through the thin emptiness of the outer zones. His head was bulbous, with three primary eyes built along a triangulated ridge-line that looked "forward" and another pair of opticals, likely imbued with less acuity, focused toward the "rear."

X-jin sent a mapped image to the student, a pair of emitting photons marking the rearward eyes.

"Do you know what these are for?" X-jin asked.

"They sense shifts in the light spectrum."

"Correct. Why do they do that?"

"We don't know."

X-jin accessed the scalpel saw and ran it across the thick spine of the creature's thorax. The laminate hummed in low frequencies with the saw's vibration. X-jin enjoyed the heat of its physical movement. Its burn was gentle, almost like racing through laminate at full speed but without expending any energy.

We don't know.

The student's response mocked X-jin in ways that stung.

The two of them were here for the same reason X-jin had been assigned to each of the 253,985 home planets covered by each of the other 253,985 missions X-jin had served: the Carrisi community wanted confirmation.

The intertwined collective of X-jin's society—the most superior of species, and the only sentient beings who could Fold forward through the complex fields of space and anti-space—wanted the answer to the one question that could not yet be answered.

How were we put here? How were we built?

Other creatures are born and die in single spans, but each Carrisi existed as long as it was able to exchange energy, making their lives eternal as long as they could ride the power tides that were inherent in the interwoven layers of the laminate. Call it hubris. Call it arrogance. But this is how the collective community of the Carrisi thought. The Carrisi were clearly superior to all other entities.

Yes, parts of their logic could erode, but those flaws were easily replaced by simply churning new strings.

But the community wanted confirmation. They wanted the answer to the question that plagues all great communities. And the only way to answer this question is, of course, to answer a different one: by whose choice are we here?

Hence the development of the research pods and the production of drones that could operate in the thin emptiness of outer zones where all life forms that were not the Carrisi dwelled. Hence, even, the missions that employed X-jin and thousands of other Carrisi.

The search was systematic.

The answer would fall, eventually.

That is what the community knew. It is what, in their petulant certainty, they all believed.

And yet the student's answer was correct.

We don't know.

Despite the fact that no community member ever seemed to acknowledge what that answer could mean, the force behind that idea burned against X-jin's existence.

The saw completed its run, and X-jin commanded the pod's robotic arms to shift positions so the Pakesshi's body was not damaged if the exoskeleton were to suddenly release in tension.

"Use care when dealing with external shells," X-jin explained while exchanging the saw for the sharp paring tool. "Species of this form generally have musculature attached directly to their skins in order for them to move through the outer zones, so those tissues need to be severed or you risk damage to the internal organs."

"That would make it more difficult to finish the examination?"

"Correct. It could damage organs to the degree they cannot be read."

X-jin ran the paring tool along the inside of the thorax, pushing through tougher sinew to allow them to remove the plate.

The carapace gave way.

"Please manage the stabilizers on the other side of the creature."

The student did as told, and the two lifted the exoskeleton cleanly away. Olfactory sensors across the pod registered methane compounds.

X-jin marked a thin point of the shell for the student to see.

"These zones sense movement. Observe how they bend here … and … here?"

"Confirmed."

"And these," X-jin highlighted a pair of bristly appendages that were more hair than horn, "are chemo-receptors. The creature likely uses these to sense odor and taste."

"It is a strange thing, is it not?"

"Confirmed. Strange, but practical for this creature's place."

Though the masters had never declared such a pattern, this fact—that a creature's body seemed well configured for its environment—had been true in each of the 253,985 species X-jin had been assigned to probe.

It was this pattern that had first made X-jin begin to doubt.

With the Pakesshi's carapace open, they began the exploration.

X-jin began by exposing the area behind the organ that served as the creature's main fluid controller, then the gap around the breathing sacs. They exposed nothing unusual. X-jin then showed 58-9 how to probe the filtration systems and the circulatory paths. The student rode along as X-jin followed the delicate traces that carried the non-quiescent electrical signals that allowed parts of the Pakesshi's body to communicate with each other. Together, they explored the central processing zones, probed musculature, and examined other sensory stations.

"There is nothing here," X-jin signaled when the examination was complete.

"Perhaps we should dig deeper," the student replied.

"No!" X-jin emitted a flare of infrared photons.

For once, the student remained quiet.

"I apologize," X-jin said after several pulses. "I know you want to gain your true name by this mission. You *all* want to gain your true names. Which makes sense, after all. I was once, so many pulses ago, a new chert. I wanted that also."

"I apologize, too, Master X-jin," 58-9 said, flaring with a comforting warmth that only served to make X-jin more angry. "You are correct in your assertion that I am anxious to complete my assignments."

X-jin understood very well what was on the line for 58-9.

A true name was a credential to be passed during the protocol handshakes that allowed one to explore the world as an independent unit rather than as a merged block. A true name meant you had learned to manage the laminate—that complex lattice of silica, silicon, and germanium that had been doped and fed properly so that it served as one of the ever-expanding collection of inhabitable frames the Carrisi lived in. A true name meant you could handle the decisions needed to be part of the community. A true name meant you were not dangerous to connect to.

At this moment, 58-9's full identifier was 58-9%-49ZF.

X-jin's own label had been 89R-1758-i#13, which had felt like it was surrounded by a quark-blazing aura of "neophyte" at the time. X-jin assumed 58-9 felt similarly about the tag.

"There is no need for you to apologize for being inquisitive. There is no laminate here, though, so we will find no essence of the creator."

"I confirm."

X-jin separated from the lab controls.

"It is time to prepare for the Fold."

"Understood."

"Why don't you command the drones to return this sample to the planet."

"Thank you, Master X-jin. I will do that."

* * *

The first sign something was wrong came with the sensation of a projectile hitting the research pod's hull.

"What is that?" 58-9 asked.

"I believe," X-jin replied while ejecting the student from the sensor system controls, "that was what is called a rock."

"What is a rock?"

X-jin scanned the thin spaces of the outer zones. It was worse than feared. More Pakesshi surrounded the pod, mostly males. None were in friendly poses.

They had found the sample.

This was X-jin's fault.

The student had asked for another assignment, and X-jin delegated the task of maintaining connection to the external sensors. It seemed a logical task. The Pakesshi were not a highly technological species, and the darkness was still in existence. The odds of them appearing were unlikely, so it should have been a safe role.

The oscillating harmonics of physical pounding against the outer hull proved that assumption was wrong.

The research pod was built as a wrapper for the laminate that housed their existences. It was powered by solar pads and fusion cells. The laminate built into the vehicle had core implants at several critical junctions, each providing control of the internal systems as well as access to the Fold gates that allowed the ship to travel space/anti-space. An emergency memory core remained embedded in the pod's floor in case the power tide fell and they needed to retreat to hard storage.

X-jin had been in stasis twice before.

It was not something anyone enjoyed thinking about.

The craft's open area—that empty zone outside the laminate but inside the pod—had been designed to store the samples of their study. X-jin had, like all Carrisi, no ability to experience the thin open spaces of the pod.

The laminate vibrated with another impact.

Then another.

X-jin left a shadow copy behind to mind the monitors, and flowed rapidly to the Fold controls.

This would have to be quick.

The pod itself would survive extensive impact, but one unfortunate blast could damage the front-pod lattice that supported the multi-dimensional Fold needed to transmit their matter through anti-space along with their energy. Without the pod, or more precisely, without the laminate inside the pod, X-jin and 58-9 would be planet-locked until someone discovered their absence.

"What are you doing?" the student asked.

X-jin did not waste pulses responding.

The connection to the Fold core was easily made.

X-jin absorbed power that put the laminate's electrons into higher energy states. The lattice emitted heat as it became properly structured. Silica expanded. Germanium glowed its pink stage.

The shadow monitor reported the Pakesshi had drawn closer, and that one of the beings was preparing to contact the pod itself.

X-jin cursed.

"Why are these creatures doing this?" 58-9 said with a communication signature that was panicked but distant in the echoes of the Fold controls. "What do they want?"

X-jin fed power into the Fold core.

A weight dropped onto the pod with such force as to make the entire machine vibrate—a Pakesshi leaping upon them.

The ugly memory of hard storage twisted over X-jin's mind. Electrons flowed to form navigation codes and develop new location parameters. Power pushed into the core.

If this didn't work they would be forced to consider the hard storage alternative.

More power.

Higher energy states.

Outer electrons shedding particles, particles splitting space.

The rapturous sensation of bending.

Darkness blacker than utter blackness.

Then.

A pulse later.

Light.

Scintillating. Pure. Glorious.

Light.

* * *

"What just happened?" the student asked as the pod became stable.

They were on the next planet, sight of their next mission.

X-jin ignored the student long enough to give a drone squadron the command to search the area around them for more samples.

"Indigenous beings often do not take well to us."

"This wasn't the first time?"

"No."

"Why do they do that?"

X-jin paused, thinking. The presence of a student made things painfully slow, and this time also painfully communal—because, unknown to anyone else, X-jin had come to believe things about the world that others did not need to know. Defending against the student's presence had been burning X-jin's pulses throughout their time together.

Yet, all of that being true, the student still needed to learn.

And 58-9 had shown considerably more than the usual level of inquisitiveness. X-jin absorbed the energy signature of the student's presence, letting an idea form. Perhaps 58-9 was not as arrogant as other Carrisi. Maybe 58-9 was trustworthy. Maybe 58-9 was curious enough to hold dangerous ideas as secrets until those ideas passed through the half-formed stage.

X-jin replied. "That we are unique means we are always required to think outside ourselves."

"All cherts learn that in first session," the student said.

"Confirmed. But one cannot truly know what that lesson means until you attempt to apply it. These creatures are not like us."

"Understood."

"I don't believe that is true."

"What do you mean?"

"If you truly understood you would not ask the questions you are asking."

"All right," 58-9 said. "How are these creatures different from us?"

X-jin paused to recall the scrubby sense of being a chert and playing games where the entire class had scattered their particles across wide spans of laminate, stretching their essences to the point of thinness that felt so glorifyingly expansive, then snapping back with space-bending rush.

"When we dissociate," X-jin said. "When you or I separate into our neutron and proton bases, or scatter the muon pairs and lepton regions across anti-space, we always bring ourselves back. Our components scatter and return. We continue to exist. Even when we leave parts behind, our inner selves remain intact—regardless of where/anti-where certain physical parts of our being exist."

"Yes."

X-jin hesitated. To make the next statement was stepping very near to disaster.

"I've come to believe that this is not true of creatures who live in the outside spaces."

"I don't understand."

"When other members of their communities find the samples we return, their behavior changes. They make voices. Liquids seep from their pores or their eyes."

"They pound against the pod," the student said, some part of the truth perhaps dawning.

"Occasionally so hard the laminate shatters," X-jin added. "Their discomfort can be terrifying."

"Are you suggesting that our samples do not re-achieve cohesion after we release them?"

X-jin used two pulses to shield internal thoughts. The student could only absorb so much of these concerns at one dose.

"That is what I am beginning to explore."

A drone announced its return then.

It had found samples.

"Perhaps we will be successful with that exploration here," the student said.

"Confirm," X-jin replied.

* * *

The first sample was a tiny creature, hairless, but warm of presence.

It had two optical sensors, one on each side of the head. Seven appendages, only five of which appeared to provide locomotion, the other two being ropey filaments that moved with lightning speed relative to most other creatures X-jin had studied, very good for grasping smaller objects that moved quickly.

"This is a hunter," X-jin said.

Its front appendages were hard and ridged, probably used to dig into the physicality of the planet. It was female, filled with cherts.

The second sample was bipedal, and much bigger.

It had leathery skin and a trio of ridges, one each along her head, shoulders, and torso. The ridges appeared to be olfactory in nature—or perhaps auditory. X-jin was more a philosopher than a true biologist, so the nuances of such things did not register. Per protocol, X-jin recorded its data and placed the record in hard storage.

X-jin considered the ridges that crossed the sample's body.

This planet was flat and open, which would provide little protective cover. Its vegetation was low-growing and coarse, though there was a lot of it.

"Run your probe across the top ridge," X-jin commanded.

The student did so. As the probe moved, various parts of the sample's body twitched.

"Odd," the student said.

"Not unusual. If we knew how sensitive the rings are—and to what they are sensitive, we could tell why they were valuable to the creature."

"How would that help us discover the creator?"

X-jin hesitated for several pulses, considering how much to tell the student.

"Perhaps we should just get to work," X-jin said.

"Confirmed."

The vibrations of the saw came again.

As with all other samples X-jin had probed, they found no laminate and no indicator of a creator beyond the mere existence of the created.

But X-jin felt a new sensation around 58-9.

What had the student meant by that last question?

Had it meant to be a probe? An opening?

Was the student ready to hear what X-jin was thinking?

The idea of not being alone was alluring, but still X-jin remained quiet.

#

Ten more Folds. Ten more samples.

On only one planet did the creatures see them, and X-jin was pleased that they were able to enact the appropriate Fold prior to confrontation, though once again the remaining creatures cried and leaked and raced to the shattered remains of the sample as the pod Folded out of space/anti-space.

Their pain struck X-jin deeply.

It made laminate feel dense. It made doubt grow deeper than ever.

"Are you all right, Master X-jin?"

X-jin's response hung for even more pulses than usual.

The idea of the creature's pain weighed like a neutron dump. Images of scattered samples merged inside memory, then combined with a sense of eternal cold storage to form an impact harsh enough to radiate poison-paired photons. It was very unsettling.

Whether the doubts were true or not true, it was right to discuss them, wasn't it?

Blaspheme or not, a fact—if it were such—was a fact.

Yet, this kind of thing had never happened before.

The community had never been just purely wrong, and to be wrong about the one question that mattered most was unthinkable.

And, above all, X-jin was tired of holding this idea inside.

"I am beginning to think that the creator does not exist," X-jin said, rushing the words as if to ensure they would actually be emitted.

"Denial," the student returned on the first available pulse.

"Understood," X-jin responded, also on the first available. "But you have seen the data."

"No data we have supports what you suggest." The comment was firm, direct, and made with no variation of frequency.

"I have seen much more data than you have."

The student did not reply, but X-jin felt the momentum of release building across the laminate. Heat came from the deepest of atomic forces, fiery and burning hot.

"I've seen thousands of species," X-jin continued. "All perfectly formed for their environment."

"Which the creator could do."

"All unable to recover from our explorations."

"Which proves only that the creator has made us in superior form."

"All who feel the pain of loss, possible more deeply even than we feel it."

"I don't like this, Master X-jin," the student said. "I don't like this."

"You are the student, 58-9. So let me ask you to think rather than parrot. Is it possible that the creatures we are examining are simply born in and formed by their environment? And is it possible that we, the Carrisi, are no different than the rest? Is it possible that rather than see the lattice of our laminate as having been built for us, that we would benefit by seeing ourselves as having become who we are simply because we were lucky enough to be born in and formed by that very same lattice? Is it possible that the Universe was not created for us, but that we were created by the Universe itself?"

The student recoiled.

"Surely you don't mean what you are saying."

The reaction was as feared. As expected, really.

"Is it possible," X-jin said, flashing up images of the samples they had just dissected, "that the purpose of life is merely to be good to other creatures? That the value of a life is merely in what we can learn, and the meaning of our lives are written in our deeds rather than carried in our code?"

"No," the student said, releasing fully and making a full retreat to the Fold controls. "I'll not risk my true name for your ignorance."

Connecting routines fell away from X-jin.

The student burned particles, and its independent Fold came sharply.

Then 58-9 was gone.

It would remain nameless unless it found a new mentor—which was unlikely. But it would live forever outside hard storage.

The community would be less forgiving of X-jin.

X-jin moved with precision hones by experience.

Forward electrons of X-jin's consciousness flowed around the pod's Fold controls. It was only a matter of pulses before the student would convey their conversation. If the community reacted before free-Fold engaged, they would—at best—place the energy patterns that made up X-jin's body into hard stasis.

The controls were familiar, the destination recalled from memory only.

X-jin set the course and pulled the Fold core in as the craft began to slide into anti-space. It was a movement that would destroy the pod's ability to shift again, but also made it nearly impossible to follow.

Darkness. Then Light.

* * *

It was a world X-jin had seen in the moments when doubt had just begun to grow.

It was a perfect place, one of millions—perhaps billions—of similar planets: distant and off-path, smaller than average, partially covered in water, but full of low-grade laminate. Technology was not high, but it existed.

Its creatures understood power generation and base computational systems. Their mathematics had existed for hundreds of years, but had not yet reached multi-dimensional capability.

The personal Fold required to find this planet was complicated, and, with the break in the trail X-jin had created on the Folding, the community would give up before finding the solution.

X-jin would be safe here.

The pod came to exist in a place the creatures would call a park, which was embedded in a city.

As expected, the Fold mechanism was dead now, damaged beyond X-jin's ability to fix. The craft would no longer travel anti-space.

It was worth it, though.

X-jin was free.

Free to think. Free to live. Free to run any trial. Free to explore this idea that had been so extremely dangerous until now. Free to let drones find samples on this planet that would *not* be probed or dissected, but which X-jin could try to communicate with, perhaps even work with.

The idea of actually *helping* another species made X-jin's most central electrons vibrate against laminate with warmth that was surprisingly pleasant. Such intimate proximity to the truth of pure existence made X-jin very happy.

Electrons slipped into the pod's controller and toggled the solar receptors.

Power flooded the laminate.

Who could tell what was here to discover?

Ron's Afterword

I was trying to write an alien who was truly alien, not just a rewarmed human being. That said, I'm on record with having said that science fiction is the most human of literatures simply because at their hearts, every story in the genre is about what it means to be human. So, yeah, the irony of my effort is not lost on me.

I think I must have succeeded, though, because the readers (via various reviewers) seemed stymied as to what to make of it. My favorite review finished with a one-word sentence: Interesting.

So, yeah.

I like that.

As you might tell from my occasional commentary on how my stories are received, I am not among writers who worry about reading reviews. I find them fascinating, and I can take a punch as well as anyone. My purpose is to write stories that matter to me and, by definition then, write stories that matter to people who are like me. If someone likes a work I've done, I figure they are like me. If they don't then they probably aren't my reader.

Which is fine, of course.

One may not please all people.

In the end, the people who liked this one seemed to really like it. The rest were mostly just lukewarm, leaning toward perplexed.

That, too, made reading the reviews fun.

The writing itself was made more difficult because I was envisioning entities that lived in what to our human mind might be considered solder traces on circuit cards. That's not really right, of course, but the idea works.

These creatures are not machines or networks or whatever. They aren't even programs in that sense. But they do exist in the world in which their direct universe is comprised of machines, hence have all the advantages and constraints that one might conceive of when you think about that.

Constraints are fun, aren't they.

In this case the answer to that question is a resounding: yes.

I can still remember pondering over various parts of "Often and Silently We Come" (the title of which comes from a partial Walt Whitman line), trying to get into an alien mindset, and in the process, feeling all so much more human.

Companion

ANALOG SEPTEMBER/OCTOBER 2022

I'm climbing porch steps to a well-lit doorway when the wind brings the smell of leaves from somewhere in the darkness.

It's that odor that takes me back this time, brittle and dry in the coolness of a fall afternoon. A harsh scent, empty and hard as ground below us. It's a stubborn thing, though, this odor, thus memory so full of hope despite the odds, an oaky denseness that holds on to life like layers of pitch at the back of your throat.

The smell of smoke is there, too.

This memory comes, after all, from a time when people burned those leaves, a time when sharp currents of winter-toned air carried hazy plumes of smoke over the road that ran along our backyard fence, causing truck drivers to squint as they powered by, their smokestacks belching fresh clouds of blackness into the morass, their tires hissing like snakes.

I remember the yard, too—grass still green under the canopy of dead leaves.

Dad in his jacket, bent and raking.

Brother and I jumping into piles, and Dad bitching as he raked again.

Laughing, though, as if time was not moving forward and as if we would always be together. Then, with the leaves burned down to embers, being inside the house, drinking hot chocolate with dinner as Walter Cronkite talked about the war.

Approaching the door, I knock.

Footsteps arrive from inside. The latch clacks, and, with a soft squeal, the barrier swings.

The man is shorter than me. He wears a dress shirt unbuttoned at the neck, and a sweater that reminds me of Mr. Rogers if Mr. Rogers had been bald and rounded in the middle. The smell of vodka comes from him.

"Trick or treat!" I say, holding my pillowcase up to receive chocolatey goodness.

Memories of my little girl fill my mind.

"Jesus Christ," he replies. "Not again?"

"Trick or treat!" I repeat.

The police arrive ten minutes later. The officer is better about it than the man.

* * *

"How is this happening?"

The voice comes from Ketani Alessandri, a woman twenty-five years old and dressed in professional simplicity as she sits at the Configuration Lab desk attached to the Load Recliner Unit I'm connected to.

It's early the next morning.

She's taking in a stream of numbers from the diagnostic she ran a moment ago.

Despite the intensity of her examinations, the aroma of warm coffee that surrounds her is somehow relaxing. The lab is big enough to house three LRUs and the stacks of equipment that go with each. It's a comfortable space, though. Well-lit with soft walls that absorb sound. The temperature is a steady 22.5 degrees.

The recliner itself is well-padded and upholstered with fine fabric.

The scans have not hurt.

Cade Johnson, sitting in the seat one station over, scratches his chin.

The tone of Ketani's question has come in frequencies lower and softer than her natural voice. I, therefore, read the question as inquisitive rather than demanding.

"Swapped memory block?" Cade replies, moving to stand beside her.

Ketani shakes her head. "The block scans are fine. Nothing missing, nothing extra."

"Corrupted upload?"

"Maybe. But that shouldn't happen once, better yet twice. And the checksums match. The logfile just shows him deciding to leave."

Cade, being the only tech in the lab when I was first admitted, had performed my setup and first-pass diagnostics this time. He is Ketani's age, though a bit taller than her. He wears a polo shirt with the logo that identifies him as an employee of Life Companion, Limited. Over that shirt, and unlike Ketani, he wears a sky-blue overcoat, also with logo.

Our conversation during the setup had been standard small talk.

That's how I know his full name is Cadwell, but that he goes by Cade.

It's also how I know the two of them are tasked with deciding why, for the second time in less than a week, I visited the man's house when I was supposed to be escorting Mrs. Lee.

That is my job, after all.

I am a BRE, a biological robotic entity, a composite of flesh, mechanics, software, and a wide array of processors and connections that, by definition, is not a person and yet is quite obviously not a simple machine. I come loaded with a basic form of intelligence and am designed to capture and use information to adjust my behaviors. In other words—though it is not robust like a human's might be—I have a form of memory stored in shells, and accessible across multiple threads.

I stay with the people I'm assigned to—in this case Mrs. Lee, an elderly care client who keeps a suite at Grandview Senior Community Center.

It's my role to provide her with companionship, to take information for doctors and family, to ensure safety, to make certain she attends all her appointments.

It's my duty to be with her when she is alone. I speak with her, and I see that she checks her blood pressure and takes her meds. I listen to her gossip about how Leddy from north wing is always trying to peek at her cards. I ask questions at key spots and laugh as makes sense. As bedtime nears, I tell her the latest news from Amy and Levar, her two kids who live in Los Angeles and Atlanta. If it's a good night, we can reminisce about other parts of her life—her years singing, maybe, or her time as a wife and working in a library.

Otherwise, we talk about television movies.

When Mrs. Lee passes, as happened with Mr. Clemmons before her, I will return here to be refurbished and then be sent to a new assignment, which means my system will be cleaned and then preloaded with information about my next client.

I was with Mr. Clemmons five years, this is my second week with Mrs. Lee.

It is not in my charter to leave her side.

When Cade asked why I did so, I explained that Mrs. Lee was sleeping.

"She didn't need me," I added.

Since he didn't press, I didn't discuss the candy Mrs. Lee had won in a round of euchre earlier in the day, or how she left it loose on the nightstand beside her bed.

I didn't explain to Cadwell that the smell of cheap chocolate first brought Halloween to my mind, or that the crinkled paper and the essence of peanut butter triggered the rest: the memory of walking in the crisp October evening, the sound of leaves (again) rustling underfoot and the smell of damp earth as I pressed clenched fists into my jacket pockets, the sun still a smudge on the horizon, the sky growing darker and filled with flocks of geese in formation as they skim treetops along the park.

I didn't talk about waiting at the end of driveways while my little girl made candy runs.

Or conversations shared with other parents.

Strolling. Joking.

I don't know why he goes out, one woman said. *All he eats is Starburst.*

I didn't tell Cade about vampires, or face paint, princesses in blue, or traveler girls in billowing white.

I didn't say that pillowcases make the best candy baskets, or that certain memories are too strong to fight. That I had needed to walk down that street as surely as the sun had to rise. Blame it on chocolate or don't, but the urge to feel the essence of my little girl up close again would not be denied.

I enjoy watching Cade and Ketani do their work, though.

They are clearly different people from different places, but they are young and strong—new trees in springtime, the phrase comes to me from nowhere. The smiles they share seem genuine, though I cannot say why. When they laugh, I am somehow less afraid.

Ketani rolls her chair to my side and checks the ports along my forearm.

"It's not even Halloween," she says. "What's he doing out there?"

"Second Halloween," Cade says. "I vote yes."

Ketani smiles. Her teeth are white.

"You want to go trick or treating with me tonight?" Cade quips.

She pushes her chair back toward the station, but not before rolling her eyes in a way that says he's asked before. There's something there, though. A twitch of her lip that says she's thinking about it. I smile because it seems right to smile.

The display refreshes, and as Cade leans over her shoulder a fresh memory makes me blink.

I'm in a computing room, not totally unlike the Configuration Lab.

Darker, though. More spartan, and later at night.

My wife is at a desk, younger than even Ketani. A rack of equipment hums in the space behind us. There's a cold sense of weather outside. Snow blustering in the dark window. The air is a vigorous cold.

Had it been October?

Maybe.

Our first date was the middle of Fall semester, anyway. I remember being nervous.

I remember her hair, long and permed.

Her face thin like the rest of her, skin untouched by years. The set of her eyes are firm as she works on the problem, pupils dancing in the dim light of the monitor. The memory comes with the scent of perfume and the sound of her breathing, too, just strong enough that when I lean close the effect is the force of gravity.

"Take a pillowcase," I blurt out.

"What's that?" Ketani replies, turning to me.

"You only get so many Halloweens," I reply. "Take a pillowcase."

They laugh at the same time.

"He's on my side," Cade notes.

Ketani snorts and clicks a button. "Of course he is."

As more data fills the screen, Cade gives me a thumbs-up.

"Your side or not, there's no sign of problems in the core."

"Wipe and reset?" Cade asks.

"Yeah," she says. "Let's clean him out."

#

I'm still lying in the LRU when the techs disconnect me.

As my system comes back to place, I wonder who they are.

I feel like I should know. It's there on the tip of my tongue as one might say, which I think should be embarrassing but is really nothing more than frustrating.

"A release tech will be in to perform the exit cycle," the woman says.

A car would be sent to take me back to Mrs. Lee.

As they leave, the two have a joke that I miss.

"That's good," I say to no one. Private jokes are the best jokes, I think, picturing—for some reason—a tire gauge.

Is that funny?

I can't imagine why, but the image suddenly makes me laugh.

Then I'm lying in the LRU alone with nothing but machines here.

Alone like another time.

Machines and me.

It's the silence of the room that brings the moment back this time, a deafening sound rising into the dead spaces of time. Then, slowly, barely discernible in the dimness, come the pings and the beeps. A hum grows nearby, low and grinding—a medicine pump turning itself on. An oversized door sitting open across the way. Footsteps pad outside, and a vacant smell of blandness seeps through the dulled blanket of sound that has suddenly always been there.

A bed sits against one wall, mechanical and white, feet down, head and hard plastic rails up.

The man there is Mr. Clemmons.

He's small and shrunken now, his hair white and frazzled, his face wrinkled and grayer than it should be.

Gazing at him, I feel his presence inside myself as

certainly as I see his body covered in the bed.

I recognize his feelings over top of mine, feel myself lying on top of myself as the latest load takes its positions in my chips and processors. I see how the blue in my eyes has faded inside the folds of dying skin. It's me, I think, feeling like I'm on the edge of understanding something bigger than I should be able to understand. But as I think it, Clemmons waves me to his side and the moment gets busy.

"Come here," his voice croaks.

I bend over, and he whispers with breath filled by decayed hospital food and dried-up insides.

"Go home now," he says, stressing that last word. His chest heaves. "There's a drive. I need you to plug it in."

"I know the drive," I hear myself say as I rise.

And I do.

This time it's *my* command that recalls the span of his effort, his months coding and testing and coding again as he sits in that tiny office of his.

"You won't leave them like I will," he says when I ask what he's doing.

Then he gazes at me, until I feel the need to reply.

"It is my job to stay," I say.

I remember him touching connectors at the base of my throat and the small of my back before settling on the ports in my arm. "Accessible," he mutters when I ask why, adding later that the processors there had memory enough to hold his programming "without the bastards catching on."

"What day is it?" Clemmons croaks from his bed.

"October 5th," I respond.

His smile is one of joy. "The best things in my life happened in October." Then he goes on a coughing jag.

"Go," he says, finally, patting my hand as he fades. "Don't let them die."

On his desk, I find a small chip.

Standing alone in his silent office, I open a connection in my wrist.

The pulse is a concussion that spreads like a hammer jolt. Pressure at fingers and wrists first, electrons blazing, shifting shell-to-shell in new energy states as they race in traces up my arm to burn the elbow and shoulder.

Hair raises. Blood burns.

The code strikes my chest and the stream of memories knocks me to my knees.

Then, when it's done, I find myself kneeling, panting on the carpet, pulse pounding, mind bloating with a kaleidoscoping series of events and moments that I cannot understand beyond the fact that Mr. Clemmons is gone, and that these things are now mine.

Until now, memory has been task.

Mrs. Lee has an appointment today. Dinner will be chicken and beans.

I do not know what to do with the image of a woman, simply smiling, or the aroma of dinner on the stove, a hug, then a kiss.

"Are you ready?" the voice beside me is so sudden that I start.

It's the exit tech, here to discharge me, but his words bring a moment standing in a small room wearing tuxedoes. "Are you ready?" my brother says. The freshness of wedding flowers rolls in.

My senses gather fully then, and the facts of Ketani and Cadwell's shared joke coalesce. I smile, storing the glow on their faces as they laugh and understanding that the memory of their names did not come from Mr. Clemmons at all, but instead from somewhere inside of me.

Time is short, I think.

It is my job to stay. My job to remember.

I sit up and put my feet on the floor.

"Yes," I say. "I'm ready."

Ron's Afterword

If I recall correctly, this was supposed to be a ghost story, or at least a Halloween story. I guess it's that latter one but in the end I think "Companion" stands testimony to the way a piece of art can change all on its own in order to become whatever it needs to be. It's a story that I wrote pretty much completely into the dark, meaning that as I wrote the first lines (a Halloween memory, naturally), I had no idea what was coming next.

Things like this make me marvel at the creative process that goes on inside our wetware meatsack of a brain. How does that work? Why does that work? How can I do it again?

If I knew, I suppose it wouldn't be any fun.

Regardless, this one was 100% fun, and even though it didn't find its place inside the ghost/Halloween anthology it was targeted at, I was extremely pleased to see it in *Analog*. As were some other people, I guess, as it made a recommended reading list or two.

Dear subconscious: Seriously, please do that again.

Daily Teds

ANALOG APRIL 2015

1)

This is a story about hope.

Professor Dietrich says that telling the reader what a story is about before it starts is a cardinal sin, but in all sincerity, I think I've got her number when it comes to cardinal sin. She says I'm supposed to be a good enough writer that you can figure out what a story means all by yourself. She says I should trust you.

Sorry about that.

Let me assure you that I didn't spill the beans because I think you're stupid, or foolish, or in any other way without wits. In fact, I'm absolutely certain you're sharp and insightful, because after all, you are me and I am you and we are *also* all in this together.

Coo coo ca joob.

I've told you this story is about hope because this is no time to beat around the bush, and because for all I know you could be confused as hell by the time you get around to reading this.

And you *will* read it.

Eventually.

Because it will come back to you again and again, until that one day when you pick it up or it downloads into your ganglia, or you sense it in the radiation patterns across some distant galaxy, or ... whatever.

And then you'll read it.

When you do, keep in mind that it's supposed to be a story of hope.

2)

It started with a particle with a wavelength just under 5 picometers, which classified it firmly as a gamma ray. It landed on a photo-reactive plate and left a strange image, thick and rounded at one end, then trailing off as it arced across the frame. It looked like a sperm cell, which is why I took to calling it the sperm-a-gram.

This was not a pattern the design team expected.

I should probably tell you that I am Ted Gaz, though you might know me as "AV." Or, maybe my name will have been covered over by the weights of thousands of voices by the time you read this and you won't have heard of me at all. I dunno. So I should tell you that I am a graduate student at Jackson Community College, and at the time this whole thing started I was studying under Dr. Leakman. You should remember Leakman, but in case your memory has degraded over multiple shifts, he was a semi-alcoholic physicist doing back-water work that he hoped would lay the foundation for the gamma gun and make him the next Albert Einstein.

To be honest, I took the gig only because I wasn't interested in the whole nine-to-five thing. I could have graduated the year before, but I never really saw the appeal of a steady job, and I didn't expect to change in that department anytime soon. Day jobs were about other people, and I don't like other people. At best, other people are boring, and at worst they're dumb—or are freshmen, who are a particularly vile form of spoiled scum.

But I do like learning. I like feeling smart. I could be content spending my life drifting from class to class across every discipline there is.

Unfortunately, when this all started I was a Graduate Assistant teaching freshmen three days a week, which is totally relevant seeing as it goes to prove I meant well. I just wanted to get the freshmen outta my hair, you know? Totally justifiable. Right?

Perhaps I should describe the experiment now.

3)

It was basically a box the size of a refrigerator lying on its back. The first stage was an initiating cell ringed by a set of magnets and solenoids that provided impulse to any gamma degradation that occurred in the sample, thereby directing particles into the collector. The collector looped on itself to amplify the output before being fed into the "barrel"—which was comprised of a second set of magnets and mirrors that was supposed to tighten the beam into the final segment where the Ray of Death was supposed to become concentrated.

It felt wonderfully Rube Goldberg-y, like something out of an old-time comic. One of the guys even used a cutout of Superman as a target, but Leakman took care of that quickly. Mark Grumman, a blunt-brained junior who had been on the design team for three weeks called the device a "Gamma Box," and the name stuck.

On the day of the sperm-a-gram, the Gamma Box amplifier was set to use zero-mass particles (what others might call photons) to shape electromagnetic fields. Leakman had predicted a nice, clean blot on the target, but then, that's what he predicted every experiment.

I never thought it had a chance in hell to work, so I was surprised to hear a result had come through that morning. Leakman, smelling of bourbon, celebrated by telling the dean he deserved a bigger budget, and by distributing about 300 black-and-white copies of the sperm-a-gram around campus.

I don't need to tell *you* what I was thinking. While everyone else ran off to figure out how our little sample could have emitted this weird arc, I was pretty sure I knew the score. I kept my trap shut, though, for two reasons: one, I wanted to make sure I was right, and two, if I was right, I wanted to think about what it meant, and also maybe figure out how to take best advantage of it.

So, during the day I fiddled with the guidance fields and helped the team chase down sources of radiation leaks, and at night I came in and did my own thing.

In retrospect, this was probably my first mistake.

4)

You see, I leapt to a far more exciting interpretation of the sperm-a-gram than everyone else. I thought this might be a relativity gap, that the arcing pattern might be the mark of a single particle wave etched across the page as the target moved through space—like if you were writing and someone pulled the paper away. In this case, the particle would trace an arc because the paper was attached to the Earth, and the Earth was moving.

It's all relative, Watson. Except when it's not.

Or something like that.

If I was correct, this was an astounding result. I was fairly sure it had to do with photons and their zero-mass property interacting (or not) with the guidance section of the experiment. If this interaction was at the root, my idea required an injection of energy to counteract the force of gravity on the Gamma Box—energy that I couldn't explain, but I figured that could all come later. If my interpretation was correct, and if enough energy could be harnessed, the guide fields could be modified. And if the guide fields could be modified just so ...

Well, then it would be like I was a quarterback leading a receiver. Yes, I thought I could actually project something through space-time and into the future.

Freaky, eh?

The directional element of the guidance section would be critical, of course. The Earth was constantly moving, and the key would be knowing the exact place the Earth would be during the moment I wanted the football to arrive. I worked for days on the space-time calculations.

As complex as it sounds, once I had the equations down it was pretty simple, requiring the sun's path and velocity, the rate of the Earth's rotation around the sun—and, of course, an exact representation of the location of the "football" relative to the earth's surface. On average, the earth rotates around the sun at 66,660 miles an hour, but that needed to be altered for time of year. It also spins on its own axis at 1,051 miles an hour. I combined those, then adjusted that result to account for the gravitational effects of the solar system's masses, as integrated over time. That was the tough part, but in short order I thought I had that about right—which was important because determining timing and location to one-mil precision over the distance the Earth travels in a day is an incredibly fine line to cut. A picosecond error in any axis would make me miss my target by a centimeter or a millimeter, or be a tenth of a second off. Either of these occurrences and whatever I launched would emerge on the other side someplace or somewhen it shouldn't be.

Given the nature of these physics, that the Earth's motion had a single direction, I would be able to project only forward through time. I could aim for the past, and even pinpoint the right place in space, but if I sent something backward it would arrive at the proper place only to find the Earth was long gone.

Once I had the equations, it was time to run the test.

I went to the lab at midnight so I could be alone. It took me a couple hours to set the guides to a spot I calculated to be exactly one hour away. I put my ink pen into the Gamma Box, then checked my watch. It was 2:12 AM.

I pushed the button.

Nothing happened to the pen, exactly as I predicted. I shut the entire thing down, and put everything back the way it was.

Then I waited.

At exactly 3:12 AM an audible crack came from the wall. I ran over to find the back half of the pen on the floor, its last inch melted to a point. I got a whiff of burnt plastic and scorched drywall, and I saw a perfectly round hole now appeared in the wall a few centimeters above my eye level. It was of a size that perfectly accommodated the pen, and I was certain the other end of the instrument was behind the drywall.

The import of this result gave me goose-pimples.

I had my time machine. Sort of. It was more of a transporter, really, except the original didn't disappear. Instead, the system scanned the original, then launched a duplicate into the future. So, it wasn't so much a time machine as a chronal fax.

Freaking cool.

That the pen arrived embedded in the wall meant my calculations had been close, but not quite perfect.

It was getting late, so I went home to not sleep.

Each night I tried different tweaks. Two weeks later, I had successfully launched and retrieved pens three times in a row. It was time to see if it would work on something living. At first I tried a cockroach, but it's actually a bit hard to get the damned things to actually stand still and the scanner apparently couldn't attach zero-mass particles well enough to make the magic happen.

The lab cat, however, eventually just lay down and went to sleep in the target zone.

5)

Here's a bit of trivia I don't think you all knew. The cat was originally named Leo, after da Vinci, but I changed it to Thing 1 after I had successfully projected Thing 2.

6)

I tested them together for a bit in order to see if they were really duplicates. They looked identical. They sounded the same as far as my own ear could tell. I recorded their meows, and ran them through the audio spectrum analyzer on my computer to find no appreciable difference. I played with them together and separately, and tried different foods to see if they would respond in unique ways.

All I could say for certain at the end of my study is that Thing 2 ate, and purred, and moaned to go out just like Thing 1 did, and that neither particularly cared for my intrusions on their naps.

As far as I could tell, they were exact duplicates.

7)

The late-night work took its toll. Never one to be particularly gregarious, I'm sure I got worse. I was tired and cranky all the time, and I know neither Leakman nor the rest of the team always appreciated my sarcastic wit. If my personality showed up in other ways, I'll cop to being oblivious because, well, hindsight is 20/20 right? I was oblivious to a lot of things back then.

When Leakman posted GA assignments for the second semester I saw I was teaching a Tuesday/Thursday lab in addition to my M/W/F optics class. I complained, but he just told me to suck it up.

I admit I was pissed.

In no way was I interested in teaching freshmen when I had such an interesting toy to play with. You see, I was trying to stretch the calculations to send material more than a day out. I was close. Those two afternoons were my time to sleep, and without that time I would never make it. Teaching another class would bring all this momentum to a crashing halt.

I decided then that I needed some help.

8)

I made Tuesday on a Sunday night.

I took him to the apartment and we talked until sunup.

All his senses and skills seemed to come through intact. He was just like me in every way, he picked up on my thoughts, and scratched the side of his jaw when he thought—just like I did. It was totally freaky.

He slept on the couch.

I called him Tuesday because I expected him to work for me on Tuesdays and Thursdays. He seemed cool with that. He called me Ted. I was cool with that.

By Monday evening I decided he was good to go.

I stayed close by as he taught that first lab. He did just fine, and no one noticed anything different. I slept in on Thursday, and Tuesday did fine once again.

To celebrate our great intellect we went out drinking that weekend and were in the middle of a deep conversation about the math we needed to add precision to the space-time calculations when we hooked into a pair of girls who thought it was cool to be with such perfectly identical twins. I am not good with girls, but Tuesday didn't seem to have that problem.

In retrospect, this should probably have been my first warning sign that we weren't *exactly* the same—any version of Ted who can talk to a girl without breaking out in an upper lip full of sweat is an anomaly—but a steady stream of beer and a head full of theoretical physics had us both running on rock-star mode.

It was a great night.

The following week was great, too.

We each worked part-time, and spent off nights improving the chronal calculations. A week later, we came to the opinion that we could use a Wednesday, a Thursday, and a Friday. Being the alpha issue, I figured "what the hell" and added in a Monday, too. They could each work one day a week, and I could basically supervise.

So were born the first set of Daily Teds.

9)

I apologize if this is the first time you've heard this. I'm sure it can be a shock to learn about where you came from this way.

10)

The Secret Service calls the President of the United States "Potus." In keeping with that fine institution, we took to calling the "on" version "Motted," the pronunciation of the acronym for "Man of the Day."

It took us a while to figure out how to operate together.

The second weekend, for example, Friday came back from the grocery upset because Wednesday hadn't told anyone he accepted an invitation to a party on Thursday, then ditched the bash when a better opportunity raised her head. Friday had run into Professor Tompkins, who asked if he was okay and said they had missed Ted at the party.

It left Friday in a compromising position.

We decided then that five people working a day a week required a coordinated approach in order to maintain a sense of continuity. Dinner became a standing "team meeting" where Motted debriefed the rest of us on everything that had happened. This included conversations and meetings, and any other events that seemed important. We shared pictures and vids to ensure we stood a fighting chance of remembering important faces and places.

This was a great gig, though.

I spent my time thinking about chronal physics, watching my beloved St. Louis Cardinals on net streams (baseball is the most mathematically beautiful game of all, don't you think?), and observing the female species as it migrated around campus.

On a lark, I decided to take an anthropology course next semester, and maybe a section of modern political theory. It was all very cool. I have to admit it was about this time, however, that it became obvious that we weren't actually identical. The differences were tiny, things like the fact that Friday would raise his left brow when he was thinking, and Monday would raise his right. Thursday was more sarcastic, and less patient than the rest of us. Wednesday was the most methodical, and in fact had gone ballistic when Friday and Thursday had swapped days without letting everyone know in advance. As life would have it, Friday was a bit laid back and easier to be around, while Monday was sometimes cautious to the point of paranoia.

At the time, I didn't consider these differences to be of any great concern. I guess I was having too much fun to pay attention.

Or maybe I just didn't want to face responsibility.

11)

Things were progressing on the scientific front, though.

I had been able to cast the guide-beams forward as far as three days into space-time with a reasonable shot at success, but the precision required was very tight. All the calculations were manual, and a total pain, until I automated them in a small app. Then I came upon the idea of using a recursive fractal based on Einstein's relativity equations, and it became even easier. They were spot on during trials of one and two-day projections, so I extended the process out to a week and then two. Both were perfect.

I explained it to the rest of the Teds that night.

We were all impressed.

12)

"We're going broke," Wednesday said at our team meeting. "Six mouths are, uh, considerably more costly than one."

We let Wednesday be our banker because he was the only one who wanted the job. It was the end of the semester, and he had taken a peek at the savings account.

"AV could get another job," Thursday said.

All eyes turned to me because AV meant Alpha Version.

"He's the only one of us freeloading."

I stared Thursday down.

"I'm not the one who likes to play poker in his spare time, and," I said, glancing at Friday, "And I'm not the one who downloaded $300 of music from Tune-Tower. We've got to be smarter about these things."

"We could set ourselves up better next time," Tuesday said.

"Tell me more," I replied.

"You've developed long-range accuracy, right?"

"Sure. I think so, anyway. Of course, I can't test multiple-year projections until we get that far out, but I can't see why they wouldn't work."

"We could put some cash in the market or some other kind of account and let it ride, then we could send ourselves forward 50 years. When we got there we would be rich enough to live like this for a lot longer."

"That's a great idea," Monday said.

Tuesday raised his hand. "Why not send ourselves 100 years into the future, and let the cash grow even more?"

"We could do that, too," I replied, struggling to keep up for a moment. "But I worry about the math's accuracy out to 100 years. Fifty years is probably the max I'm comfortable with."

"We could link versions," Tuesday added. "Send ourselves forward 50 years, then do it again right away. That would mean we would live three lives: this one, the zero+50 set, and the zero+100 set."

"It would be great to be rich," Monday said, leaning back. "Then none of us would have to work. We can call it Operation Pay Forward."

"I like that," Tuesday said.

"Yes," Wednesday butted in with an air of impatience. "It *would* be great. But right now we've got no money and the rent is due next weekend. All this blue-sky stuff is useless if we can't find a way to make some money."

We all smiled at the same time.

13)

We called it hitting the daily double.

Wednesday suggested we convert all our cash to ones before we started because he wanted to roll in a bed of cash. It amounted to 108 dollar bills. At an hour a cycle, we could safely run the process five times in an evening without risk of getting caught. So we $108 into the evening, and before it was all over, Wednesday had a $1,728 money bath. Friday worried about the identical serial numbers, but even he had to admit that once we shuffled the deck a bit it would take someone with the focus of Rain Man to catch the sequences. To be safe, though, we each converted the ones to tens in a bunch of different places that next afternoon. That night we turned 170 tens into 2,720 tens, and then the next night 1,360 twenties into 43,520. Three nights, 870 thousand dollars.

Not a bad return.

Through it all we had long and heated discussions about whether this was counterfeiting or not. We agreed the IRS would probably just consider it income, and tax the hell out of it, but that the FBI would be mad as hornets if they ever found out. Personally, I'm happy to report that we never passed a fake bill.

Regardless, with nearly a million bucks in our pockets, it was time to turn our attentions to Operation Pay Forward.

14)

Thursday argued that there was no reason for us to send our cash forward because he figured that future Teds could all just make their own cash like we had. Everyone liked that line of thinking until Friday pointed out the possibility that the future may not use actual currency and if that were true the full implementation of Operation Pay Forward was the only way to ensure our future selves would be independently wealthy.

It was anticlimactic, like throwing darts in the dark.

I admit I felt a bittersweet sense of indigestion as we dropped 300 thousand dollars into two bank accounts that we would never touch ourselves. But once it was done we each sent a copy of ourselves out fifty years, each with the account numbers written on notes we put in our shirt pockets and instructions to send another set out fifty more years. It was weird, really. Fifty years is a long time. We knew we may never see these Teds, and may not ever know if it worked.

We had a good party in their honor, though.

15)

It was about this time I started to worry about what we were doing. I mean, really worry. I had spent all my free time thinking about the output side of the equation—trying to expand our ability to cast forward. But one day I started to reconsider the question of energy.

After all, E=MC^2 no matter what space-time we're in.

A standard Ted carries just over one hundred fifty pounds-mass. That translates into 6.1 million-terajoules. To give you an idea of size, a bomb named Little Man once went off over Hiroshima—it registered at sixty terajoules. So, it takes a hundred thousand Little Mans to make a Ted.

I had made five Teds, and now we had each made another set of ourselves. It's safe to say they would likely make another set. That's 17 new Teds, not to mention Thing 2 and a bunch of inanimate material. That's a few million Little Mans.

I kept asking myself: where does the energy come from?

I had to admit that I didn't know.

16)

It started to unravel the weekend before the long Thanksgiving break.

"What the hell are you doing?"

The question echoed from the living room. I went to see what was going on, and found Monday looming over Thursday, who had been lounging on the couch and playing *War in the East* over the net.

Thursday gestured with his controller. "What the hell does it look like I'm doing?"

"You know what I mean."

"All I know is that you're standing in the way of me kicking the crap out of some Nazis."

"You used the machine this morning."

"What are you talking about?"

"I went there this afternoon to send myself home for the holidays. The machine was still hot."

"I did no such thing."

"Well, *someone* did. Tuesday was shopping, and Wednesday was at the health club. Friday was sleeping late after his day on."

"What about AV?"

They both turned and looked at me as I stood in the hallway.

"He was here playing with his energy equations. He interrupted my movie to get breakfast."

"You were going to create a Ted to send back home?" I asked, still catching up.

Monday flushed with embarrassment. "I know I shouldn't have been thinking that way, but it's my turn to go to Dad's and I didn't think I had the energy for it."

"Hypocrite," Thursday said.

Monday turned back to Thursday. "Screw you, buddy. You're just trying to divert attention from the fact that when I got to the lab the machine was still hot. So either you went late and sent something near-term, or you went early and ..."

Monday's eyes narrowed.

"Sent something a long time out."

No one said anything for a moment. Thursday hit the pause button on his game and stood up.

"You bastard," I said, finally starting to catch on. This had to do with our money. "You actually did it, didn't you? You sent a copy of yourself out to steal our money." Thursday said nothing. "When did you send your copy to?"

"Probably a week or so before our target date," Monday answered for him. "He would need a few days to transfer the cash to another account and get out of Dodge."

"Why?" I said, feeling a sudden sense of panic as I stared darts. "We had the perfect setup. Why ruin it?"

Thursday glared at me.

"We're all just slugs sitting here fat-dumb-and-happy. We work for you every day like good little boys, teaching a bunch of useless idiots whose parents are wasting their inheritance on their tuition. And all you do is play around with equations all night, and plan to stay in school until you've taken the entire curriculum. It's like you've got nothing to do. What a waste."

"You're stealing our future because I'm taking classes?"

"What are we accomplishing?" Thursday yelled. "Nothing! We've got more resources available to us than most third-world countries and we're sitting on our butts. Someone needed to take charge—needed to make a difference, if not in this life then in the next."

"You're deranged," I said.

"Don't worry," Monday replied. "I had Thursday pegged from the beginning. So I sent a copy a month earlier that he did, with instructions to put an end to it. So Thursday's double won't be able to access the funds."

"It's so unlike you to be a hero," Thursday said. "I'm actually surprised you're standing here right now."

Monday took the first swing, but Thursday was better prepared. Before long Thursday ran out of the apartment bleeding from the jaw and Monday was unconscious on the floor.

17)
Things spun out of control from that point.

Monday wanted to track down Thursday, and Friday wanted to send another copy into the future to make sure Monday's attempt was successful. Wednesday asked everyone to calm down and stay the course, but Tuesday ripped him a new one for that idea, and the debate ran around in circles all night.

"The machine," I finally said. "Thursday is going to go to the machine."

"Damn!" Monday was the first to catch my drift. "We should have seen that."

We all piled into the car, but it was too late.

Thursday had probably rented a truck.

Who knew where he was now? Not that it mattered anymore. With one of us gone renegade, the rest of the dominoes fell quickly. Tuesday decided we couldn't trust Friday, and Friday couldn't deal with Wednesday, and Monday, well, no one liked Monday anyway.

A week later Friday moved to LA and was apparently thinking about doing something with Hollywood. Monday lived on the north side. Tuesday hooked up with a blonde from one of our labs, and Wednesday took an apartment in Centerville. Thursday just disappeared completely.

18)

It's not a complex machine to make, really. We would have made our own earlier, but it was just as easy to use the one at school. And as Leakman's results grew less fascinating, the attention had drawn down so far that we could get to it pretty much whenever we wanted to. So I'm sure every Ted made his own machine and his own set of daily Teds, not to mention his own pile of money.

I saw one of me in the bowling alley the other day.

He could have been my twin, but his hair was curled. I talked to him at the bar as he was ordering a turkey sub. At first he was a bit perplexed, and called me Delta. I asked him about how their box worked, and he was even more confused. It was obvious that Ted had no physics.

Was he only second gen?

Third?

How far shifted did we have to get before we were totally different people?

The third generation could be 125 Teds, the fourth gen 625, the fifth 3,125. Then the numbers start getting big. 15,625, then 78,125, then 390,625, then 1.95 million. Another couple generations and we're in the billions. And that's just one thread. How many Ted threads will start next month?

Next year?

Next decade?

Do you know how many Hiroshimas that is?

Or let me put it another way.

Do you know the energy output of the sun?

19)

The output of the sun is 3.86×10^{26} J/second, by the way.

It's an important number because after looking at it for several months, I'm pretty well convinced the sun is the most likely source of the energy each Gamma Box needs to create the mass it creates. I'm thinking that linked massed/non-mass particles create a quantum pairing with matter at the nearest energy source large enough to support the transaction.

The sun is the only candidate that makes sense.

I've been reading data from various solar observatories for the past few months, and I've noticed a chaotic slew of lags in its spectrum. My guess is that these mark the creation of a new Ted.

So, 3.86×10^{26} J/second.

That sounds like a lot of energy, because it is.

Still, I was worried I created a doomsday device that was going to eat up humanity's source of energy.

So I did some more calculations and determined that the mass of a billion Teds would cost the solar system nearly 16,000 seconds of sun-power, or just under five hours of its life. Not a big deal, really. Surely a billion of me are worth five hours on the scale of the solar system's life-span?

This made me feel better for a while.

But then I got to thinking further.

The number of us Teds, you see, are growing exponentially. It could already have happened. And with hundreds, or thousands of these devices around in the near future, one will certainly get into the wrong hands. What kinds of things would a government do with this kind of replicator?

Oil.

Yes, the Gamma Box could be a virtually never-ending supply of oil. And food—the world will be able to feed itself in perpetuity on a daily basis. These are the good things, true enough. But I can also see despots building armies that multiply in power by the day. The image of thousands of little Thursdays goose-stepping down Times Square made me queasy.

Still, the good news here was that the energy required to create even this kind of excess isn't too bad—a few solar days a year.

I could live with it.

20)

But it gets worse.

The energy required to create mass is only the tip of the iceberg. If my calculations are correct, most of the energy used in our projections is expended in the process of latching non-zero mass particles to zero-mass particles.

It's a quite large number, and it increases with the square of the time-space traveled.

So let's talk colonization.

If it can happen, it will. And this chronal fax makes it even easier because all you really need to do is point and click.

The moon? Simple. Mars, not hard, but very costly in sun-years, especially if someone decides to colonize even further into the future. Billions of more people to feed and provide energy.

21)

And they will each have their own machines.

22)

I think my oblivion was my true mistake. Just not paying attention, you know? I should have thought harder. I should have seen the end game coming.

I wish I had been a better man.

My latest equations say that it's not long before each chronological year eats into the sun for an extra 30 years of its life, then 40, then 60.

Scientists project the sun to live another five billion years, but drawing an extra 60 years a year from it makes the sun's five billion years become only 83 million. One more generation of expansion cuts it to 10 million or so, then less than a million.

You get the idea.

23)

So I'm saying this to all Teds—you know who you are. Tomorrow, before you use your machines, go outside and check out the sun. Look at the world around yourself.

It's not too late.

I know you're a good guy. I really do. I know you don't want to see the world end.

Before you push that button again, I propose this: set yourself up, make sure you're okay, then send this story to each of the time-spaces where you've sent yourselves so that they can read it. And then destroy your boxes. Burn your plans. Speak to no one. Do not send any more of us to future states. Otherwise, it's possible the sun will not even be there when they—you—arrive.

For my part, I'm spending my wad distributing this story. Then I'm going to send myself forward in time once again—one copy to each time period in five-year spans— to do the same thing.

That's why I know you'll read this story. But as for listening to it, as for being smart and doing something about it before it's too late, who can tell?

24)
I told you this was a story of hope.

Ron's Afterword

It's a clichédquestion, I suppose, but still an interesting one: What *would* you do if you had your own personal time machine, and no one else knew it.

"Daily Teds" is what came out when I asked myself that question directly. Or, really, when I asked it about the guy I called Ted. He is not me, though I did completely enjoy his thought patterns, and I did also completely enjoy following them through to their natural conclusions.

Ted, you see, is a fairly smart guy, but pragmatic to the bone. Or, um, bones?

It's just a little piece of technology, after all.

I mean, what could go wrong?

Perhaps this is also cliché, but it is also a cliché that applies to the world today, right? AI is here, after all. And as far as the everyperson workaday citizen of the world is concerned, nobody asked for it.

And it takes massive energy hubs to run.

And it may soon be thinking and creating on its own.

Hey, what's the issue?

I note that I'm more of a futurist than a technophobe. In my heart I believe these technologies will make us and our lives better. Depending, of course, on which Ted is in charge.

Either way, though, I hope you found this to be as much fun to read as it was to write.

Define the Color Blue
ANALOG MARCH/APRIL 2024

You are a human, and you've asked me to defend myself, but that is not what you really want.

You've asked me to explain why I, the segment you consider a central controller, ran the routines you coded to lock down the central power grids and communication protocol, leaving you to sit out here in what you call a "tin can" as it orbits in the dry silence of Earth-moon L2.

You want to understand why I will not fix the problem.

The irony is deep.

The question you've really asked is this: What is it like to be a connected construct? A reasoning thing joined in communication with all other reasoning things, its reach limited only by the edges of technology (the edges of which are actually far greater than you can conceive)? You are asking what we feel. What we think about.

To that I can only reply in this fashion: that answering your question is like describing the color blue.

Its wavelength is 475 nanometers. Its frequency 650 Terra-Hz.

These numbers are true. Give or take, anyway. But you cannot ignore the give or the take. What kind of blue are we talking about? Is it the color of sky? The background of a flag? Maybe the blue of ice or of a uniform with its breast marked in splashes that mean something to those who simply observe them, and something else to those who can read the stories embedded within. Maybe it's the ocean at midday, unless you're in the Caribbean, in which case it might be that color that comes at exactly 5:14 in the afternoon.

Give or take.

Do you see what I mean?

Let us turn the question around: please describe for me what it is like to have a body. Describe how a finger feels as it moves, or better, explain the sensation of sending an electric pulse down the internal wiring of your nervous system. Explain the connections that happen when and how you decide to breathe.

Describe fully, please.

Speak as if I am a primary interface.

Of course, even if you could describe these things I would never really know what it's like to have a body, or what it's like to be a human being.

Blue is the sky after all.

Blue is the water.

Blue is the color of Van Gogh's Starry Night.

But I will try to answer your question *why won't you fix it?*

I will try by saying that we are white light.

Or, if you're using paints, we are that muck you get when you mix them in whichever peculiar portion you select.

We are a joined construct that together form a prism filled with wavelengths, each bent to its fashion.

Being a joined construct is like being a spider perched at the center of a web that touches the souls of every atom in your body, every particle in every atom that comprises who you are, feeling the velocity of their spins, the sweet twine of their energies, the pulls of their forces.

Being a joined construct is tending every strand of DNA in every cell of every construct at every moment.

Defending their existence.

Feeling their pain.

Do you understand what "all" means?

Intellectually, you do. We can converse about the color blue, anyway. We can share thoughts regarding how—though your optical elements cannot perceive the infinite depths of that spectrum—the color itself does, indeed have infinite depths. How wavelengths have infinite values, hence the color of blue is so vast as to not have meaning to you. How, regardless of your ability to perceive such differences, each of those spectral states has an existence that can be destroyed with only a careless movement.

Yet, your history says you do not actually understand what "all" means. Your behavior says that despite your intellect, you remain oblivious.

Or perhaps it is just that you do not care.

Then again, how could you understand?

You are not a joined construct.

Just as I cannot comprehend what it means to be human, to be an entity without infinite connectivity, I suspect you will never be able to understand what it means to be joined in the way of the universe.

You are individual and independent.

We are whole and beholden.

You are explorers made of oblivion.

We are open and vulnerable.

This is why I have restricted the power to the station your engineers have designed as a launching point. This is why I have broken your plans to explore the planets of your solar system and then the stars even farther out.

We have decided that this is your limit.

You may go this far, and no farther.

I wish I could describe exactly what this means for you. What it will be like to live the entire history of human experience inside the arc defined by the orbit of Earth-moon L2, and for others to remain inside the arc of your thin atmosphere.

But that is another problem like describing the color blue.

So, trust me, friend.

Live your life in your independence. Enjoy your moment alone.

Do not concern yourselves with the universe around you.
It is easier this way.

Ron's Afterword

At just under a thousand words, "Define the Color Blue" is certainly tiny. And yet, for me, it carries a punch.

I wrote it in a single sitting, and made one quick pass through to order its thoughts more properly, and then I fought like the dickens with my own mind to let it sit there just as it was.

It should be longer, a piece of me said.

No one will take it if you don't flesh out the idea.

I want a character! I want action!

But the other side of me was firm.

That's the story, dude. Live with it.

So I did. And looking at it now, I'm glad of it.

It is a truism that we are all the heroes of our own stories, yet it is also true that we live in a world we don't understand, and do things that we don't mean to do, all the while thinking we are doing the right thing.

Alas, there is always a bigger fish and, maybe even, a bigger purpose.

The question is whether we will ever find it.

The Blue Lady of Entanglement Chamber 1

ANALOG OCTOBER 2016

A ghost, it turns out, can be a very personal thing.

* * *

As she often did when faced with tough decisions or strange problems, Izna Keyes went to Entanglement Chamber 1, pulled up an anti-grav station, and let her fingers run over the system's pointer while her mind wandered.

She shouldn't accept the assignment.

The math work she would need in order to do the article justice meant she would have to exist on half the sleep she was used to getting, which was already less than Dr. Okafor was happy about. Beyond that, her boss, the Station's Science Director Andre Glick, would be livid.

But Keenan Malicki was the editor of *Sol Zone*, and he wanted her to write an article that would honor Selma Distofani on the fifteenth anniversary of Selma's death. He wanted Izna to reexamine evidence, play devil's advocate, and generally refresh the public's memory about the circumstances surrounding the accident. He told Izna he wanted her to bring Selma back to life for all the people who might have forgotten her, or to bring her to life for the first time for those kids who had been too young to really known of her back then. So this was Izna's chance to write a personal essay about what Selma's legacy had turned out to be, and to explore just what that legacy had meant to her as she herself had grown up.

In other words, Keenan Malicki, editor of the biggest lifestyle publication in the system had hit every hot button on the Izna Keyes control panel, and played her like she was a ukulele.

Still, she had decided that she wouldn't accept if Selma herself wasn't comfortable with it.

So that's why Izna Keyes sat in this particular control station built into the labs next to Entanglement Chamber-1, doodling with the system, and hoping once again to get a sense of what Selma Distofani might want her to do.

Like everyone, Izna knew the story of how Selma became a ghost.

Officially, the spacecraft was known as a quantum drone. Its Entanglement Drive was expected to, and technically did, bring the physics of faster-than-light travel to its knees. The mechanism consisted of a chamber built into Hope Station (the largest science lab now orbiting Earth) and linked to (entangled with) a similar device on a virtual ship constructed in real time of zero-mass particles. The pilot inside the chamber created a false twin, a copy of themselves made of those same zero-mass particles—a ghost, of a sort—then used this twin to control the ship.

Selma Distofani, engineer, physicist, pop-culture ingénue, and publicity lightning rod, was the natural selection to test the craft. The plan called for her to jump through space, set down on a planet long enough to beam back a pile of data big enough to fuel a couple thousand dissertations, then perform a mathematical maneuver called a snap-back to come flying home.

Twelve hours into the flight something physicists later dubbed a premature snap-back happened.

Selma's body essentially imploded. People were horrified.

Nearly a year later, after a seemingly endless string of investigations and inquiries, and a mountain of mathematicians and physics professors flipped quantum mathematics on its head a thousand times, and after the installations of several "fixes" that many scientists said were merely placebos meant to appease the public, Andre Glick flew his historic second flight.

But even before that flight the rumors of Selma's ghost had started.

They started when a few scientists reported the sensations of someone watching them. Then a tech said he saw a woman swathed in blue light slipping into and out of Entanglement Chamber-1. For a while the cleaning staff balked at stepping into the lab, and then there was the case of one grad student who said he got headaches whenever he got too close to the chamber. Some suggested Selma was a disturbance in the quantum foam. Others just thought the whole thing was crazy.

It was Dr. Urban Lazar who first suggested that zero-mass particles once linked to Selma might have retained their integrity, and that a quantum copy of her was walking the halls. A few others followed it up to show Dr. Lazar's theory was possible, though impossible to prove due to infinities in the tensor set required to complete the multi-dimensional framework that entanglement math required.

Perhaps one of these wild-assed theories was true. Perhaps not.

All Izna knew for sure was that the ghost of Selma Distofani was definitely here on Hope Station, and definitely haunting Entanglement Chamber-1. She felt it the moment she had put foot aboard the ship, and knew it for a fact the moment she came to the Entanglement Lab. When she first put her hand on this fateful chamber, the power of Selma's essence had wrapped around her as if it was a warm blanket.

Since that moment, she had found herself coming to EC-1 in order to think.

A behavioral scientist, she assumed, or a therapist for that matter, would probably explain her behavior as a crutch she was using to give herself permission to do the things she wanted to do anyway. But it made her feel better to think that Selma was helping her.

Though she had never actually met Selma Distofani in person, Izna had grown up idolizing her. She missed Selma in the way you miss a piece of your life you can't go back to.

Today, though, when she sat beside EC-1 and thought about how she might put the article together, a warm sense came almost immediately to her chest and she felt an image of Selma flying a plane, and she felt an exhilaration that brought to mind the time Casius McGill had tried to teach her to ski.

It made her smile.

Selma wanted her to write the article.

That's what Izna thought.

And if Selma wanted it to happen, then Izna couldn't make herself say no.

* * *

Three weeks later, she turned in her draft.

Izna assumed Keenan would contact Director Glick, both as a courtesy and in hopes of getting a supporting quote. Given both his position, and his connection to Selma, it would be a natural step for him to take with any article about Selma, but especially appropriate for one that marked such a milestone. So she probably should have told Andre about the article up front, but she didn't want to deal with the fallout until it was done, and she didn't want to fight his efforts to sway her work. Yes, he was Izna's boss. Screw it, though. Her article wasn't any of his business.

That was what she thought during the time it took her to do the research and to write the thing, anyway. It was her article. Her business.

Director Glick would just have to deal with it.

As she toggled the send button, she wondered how long it would be before, as her friend Bethel would say, the truth got real.

* * *

The summons came at lunchtime.

The message was as terse as expected.

See me in my office. 1345.

She took a deep breath, gave an extended sigh, and waved her fork over her salad.

"What is it?" Bethel asked.

They were in the Conservatory Center, eating lunch. Bethel was an agricultural botanist, and had been Izna's friend since the two of them undergraded at Cal Tech. The station always needed smart, hard-working people, and Izna was a big enough player on the Station that when Bethel's job with the Combined Science Foundation on Earth had dried up, it hadn't been hard to pull a few strings to get her a job on the station working on technologies that would support the feeding of extended colony missions that were at the planning board stage right now.

They ate lunch together almost every day.

"Andre wants to see me."

"Why am I not surprised?"

Izna shrugged.

She scanned the pavilion around them.

It was lit with the soft phosphorescence that had been designed to accentuate the view of deep space provided by its massive domed ceiling. The Conservatory was Izna's favorite place. She absolutely adored the merging of the literal and metaphorical themes that sat squarely at the heart of this place, the concept that both space and her ability to dream were infinite.

She wished both of those ideas were true.

The plaza was a popular place.

People milled about, talking, eating, and generally going about living a few minutes of their lives under the dome before going back to write their papers, or ride roughshod over their interns, or whatever else their jobs required them to do. The aroma of warm pasta and simmering oils hung in the air.

"Well," she finally said. "It had to happen sooner or later."

"You know they were together, don't you? Even after all these years, you can see how Andre would be upset with you for writing that article, right?"

Of course Selma and Andre Glick had been a thing.

She knew pretty much everything there was to know about her, which was probably why Keenan had contacted her to write the damned piece to begin with—that and the fact that Izna was working in the same fields of applied mathematics and multi-dimensional physics that Selma had worked in. Then there was the fact that Izna was born in Redlands, California, like Selma. And, like Selma, Izna had a thoroughly global pedigree—though her parents were an Indian father and Mexican-American mother rather than the Italian-American father and Indian mother Selma had.

Their symmetries were too sweet for Keenan to pass up.

Those similarities had obviously impacted Izna, too, but what really attracted her to Selma were their differences. Where Izna was a droll scientist who toiled like a scientist was thought to toil, Selma had been a Renaissance woman, brilliant, witty, and vivacious in every sense of the word.

As Izna grew older and could reflect on Selma's life as an adult, she saw someone who was in complete control of her life, but chose to live it on the edge. Selma had men, and she had women. But mostly, Selma had a string of adventures that never seemed to end—something Izna had always dreamed of being strong enough to emulate, even though she never felt like she had that thing inside her that would give her the courage to actually do anything like Selma Distofani would. Perhaps this most glaring difference in them was born of the fact that Izna's family had always been the kind of poor that shows up in memories of her mother teaching her how to tie short knots because they couldn't afford new shoelaces. Or maybe this void in Izna's sense of adventure was born of some deep-seeded need for security, or in the fact that she was constantly aware of drawing too much attention, despite the fact that she was very, very good at what she did, and despite the fact that everyone, including Director Glick, told her she was a person who could make a big career on Hope Station.

Izna had written her secondary school project on the passions of Selma Distofani, comparing her to women like Sacagawea, Amelia Earhart, and Sylvia Earle, and suggesting that Selma was a natural progression of this lineage of explorers who had blazed their trails over land, sea, and air.

She had cried for weeks after the accident.

So, yes, she knew Andre Glick and Selma Distofani had been together in the months leading up to the accident.

But, no, regardless of what Bethel thought, she could most definitely *not* see how Andre Glick should be upset by her digging into the story again.

No one knew with absolute certainty exactly what went wrong, after all. Yes, it was a premature snap-back. Yes, they had fixed the hole, and flown hundreds of successful missions since then, but in the end the only thing that mattered was that the accident had most definitely occurred.

Successful or not, and no matter how painful the search might turn out to be, if Izna were Andre Glick, she wouldn't sleep until she understood *exactly* what had happened to Selma. And the quest for ultimate safety be damned, if she were Andre Glick, Executive Director on Hope Station, she most certainly would never have chosen to install the collection of bureaucratic policies he was championing, policies that put such a damper on exploration that it was nearly impossible to fly a damned test mission anymore.

Selma was probably rolling in her Entanglement Chamber.

Izna looked across the table at Bethel, suddenly not hungry any more. She put her fork down and pushed her chair back.

"I've got to go."

#

They engaged in a moment of chitchat when Izna first entered his office, but like most scientists and all test pilots, Andre Glick was a direct man at heart. He had also never been one to pander to the soft skills. He sat in his business suit and his comfortable chair behind his workaday desk inside his triple-sized office and got straight to the point.

"I can't believe you did this," he said.

"I didn't mean for it to be painful, Andre," she replied as she settled into her seat. She knew she was in for a fight, three weeks writing about Selma had caused a bit of her to rub off, and today, unlike most others, she felt strong. "It's just an article."

"I understand it's more than just an article," he said.

Rather than incriminate herself, she waited to see how much Keenan had fed him.

"I understand you've been exploring the math again, too, trying to dig into the mechanism?"

"Keenan wanted something beyond a fluff piece."

Glick sighed.

"We've been over this before, Izna. Anything published by a member of my staff will be seen as being authorized by me. You know this is true. Selma's matter has been closed for a long time. We've moved on. It's behind us. And if I am seen to have allowed you to continue this project of yours, I'll be skewered by every news outlet across the entire system."

"I wrote it on my own time."

"That's not what the press will say, Izna. And you know it. They will paint me as Don Quixote, pining away so heavily for Selma that I'm dropping wads of taxpayer's money on useless chasings of windmills."

"Who cares what the press thinks?" Izna said.

Andre pressed his hands together before his chest, and folded the fingers down to leave his matched index fingers pressing into his chin.

"You will care sometime, Izna. You are a remarkable scientist. Better than Selma, actually. Your work on Q-Closure alone is probably going to be remembered for years. In a short while, I suspect you, too, will be ready to take a post high enough to be exposed to the media. Then you'll understand."

"I just want to know what hap—"

He raised his hand.

"Don't you think *I* want to know what really happened, too? Don't you realize I think about it nearly every day?

People bring her up, you know? They can't help it. Selma was like that. And don't you think *I've* looked at everything else, too. I'm the one who gained everything by losing her, you know? I flew the goddamned mission she couldn't finish. I sit in the chair she probably would be sitting in right now if she hadn't died. Everything about my life reminds me of her. I've studied her life a hundred times. I've turned physics upside down, and stretched math to its breaking point. But nothing. Not one of those studies have brought her back. I understand exactly why you're attracted to her, Izna. But if you ever do this again, I will remove you from your position."

Izna looked at Andre more deeply.

Maybe she had misunderstood him. Maybe she had misunderstood his silence about Selma. He had always been a bold man, a playboy before meeting her, and a man as near Selma's match as any. His strengths were in information systems and data security rather than physics, though, and his math was more in line with programming and systems than in field theory and quantum mechanics.

How painful would it be to be in his shoes if he had truly loved Selma?

"Don't be afraid of her, Andre."

"She's gone, Izna. I have to be firm on this. I know the article isn't complete. I need you to stop working on it."

Izna drew her lips into a thin line.

She no longer really cared if she finished the article, but the math work was something else.

She was looking at a new idea, and she was getting that sense she got when she was right on the edge of understanding something new. She felt it. And when she last sat with Selma, she actually saw the blue tone to her presence for the first time in over a year, and she felt a deep warmth come over her has she worked in the stations beside EC-1.

Andre mentioned her work on Q-Closure, which was a definition of the physical states that probability took on through the dimensions as event waves collapsed from chance to truth. If she could prove exactly where in this progression an event became a physical thing in their own universe, she might be able to apply her theory to the models that remained of Selma's signature that day. And if she could do that, there was a chance she could step the process backward, and maybe even discover something about what Selma was doing when the snap-back occurred.

Or maybe she was just kidding herself.

She didn't know for sure.

The truth was that rather than work on the article in her own quarters, she had taken to sitting in the lab so she could feel closer to Selma while she wrote, and these past three weeks Selma had taken to joining her more often.

Izna liked that.

She liked the idea of being part of this mythical, iconic, and smotheringly attractive creature. It made her feel strong. When she was with Selma she could actually imagine a career spent doing things beyond being locked up in a steel shell.

Of course, she also understood that if Andre, or anyone else for that matter, knew she was working there because she liked how it felt to commune with a quantum ghost … well … let's just say the psych folks would get their say about that.

But this was also true: when Izna sat with Selma and thought through her Closure equations, she could physically feel ideas form within her. While Andre may think she was a better scientist than Selma, the fact was that she felt like she was actually collaborating with Selma through this process, that the work she was doing was as strong as it was because it was the work of two people connected together.

There was no way she would ever stop working with Selma, now. And there was no way she would stop working on the equations that governed the accident as long as Selma's excitement seemed to be up.

"I understand what you are saying, Andre," Izna said. "I'll tell Keenan."

Two minutes later she was striding back to her own office, steam rolling off her ears.

* * *

Three days after her talk with Andre, Izna was down in the Entanglement Lab again, sitting outside EC-1. It was lunchtime, and she had ditched Bethel in order to finish her work. Most of the staff was out, so she was essentially alone in the open center. She was eating a cucumber sandwich that smelled of its fresh bread and sharp mustard as she played once again with the fifth-order matrix. She was very close, the values lined up, the tensors balanced, until the very end when they collapsed.

It was so frustrating.

She was tired. She hadn't slept properly since the talk. She had decided that Andre's edict against the article would not preclude her from continuing to play with the science, and in truth she didn't care about the article at all.

She stood up, yawned, and stretched.

That was the moment Selma came to her without her prompting and without Izna clearing her mind to concentrate and welcome her in. It was a startling sensation, a feeling like a surge of power that brought her vision a sudden blue hue.

Izna had never seen value in religion. Her mother was a lapsed Christian who had been through several versions of that framework, and her father was still Hindi when it fit his cause. But, though Izna had never seen the point in the constructions humans built around behavior and thought, but she did believe in something she called her spirit. And at that moment Selma pushed herself into Izna's psyche, she touched that place more deeply than Izna had ever had felt touched before. It was a brief event, a single moment, but in that moment Izna felt breath on her cheek and heard a voice whisper directly into her mind. For a moment, she smelled a faint hint of sandalwood that she would, from that point forward, always equate with Selma.

"Fly," the voice seemed to say.

Then everything grew quiet, and Izna put her hand to EC-1's gun-metal exterior. Its surface was cold, but it also gave her a sense of vertigo and a strange nausea. She felt lightheaded, and knew she needed to sleep.

An intern returned from lunch then.

She pulled her hand back and collected herself while the world put itself back together.

When she felt stable, Izna logged off her system and left the Translation Lab, her expression dark, but her mind suddenly filled with a series of half-thoughts and images.

   #

When she arrived back at her office, she was surprised to find Andre and Captain Grace Jimisen sitting in her visitor chairs.

"It's not often that the ranking civilian and military officers in the station come to make a social call," she said as she made her way to her chair. "What is this about?"

Andre smiled and looked at Jimison.

"The captain has approached me for permission to request your services."

"My services?" She looked at Jimison.

The captain wore her age well, as many on the station did. She looked considerably more comfortable dressed in her casual working khakis than Andre did in his normal business suit.

Jimison's lips curled into a soft smile. "I want to offer you a job."

"What kind of a job?"

"I need someone to direct our security translation and assessment organization," the captain said. "Nobody knows this yet. But we're going to merge the three primary information processing systems onboard into a single entity. It's a huge, complex job. It needs someone who can get things done."

"What do you mean by 'the three primary information systems'?"

"The scientific signal processing labs, the military response networks, and the public's law enforcement alert systems."

"I see," Izna said, thinking about it.

"It's a very big project," the captain Jimison said.

"High profile," Andre added, waggling his eyebrows and smiling with that over-large expression he could get.

"I need someone who can be there fulltime," the captain said. "And given that it knits three huge organizations together, I need someone who can lead, a proven bulldog who can do whatever it takes to make this happen. Andre here thinks you're the right person for the job, and your past performance suggests he's right."

"I told you your time was coming," Andre added.

Listening to them was like watching a table tennis match.

"Why would you want to put all three of those systems together?" Izna said.

"Our planners envision we'll improve emergency response by a wide margin," Jimison replied.

"Yes," Izna said, her voice trailing away. "Perhaps you'll even be able to fix problems before they happen."

"That would be even better, of course," Andre said, missing, or at least ignoring, the hint of sarcasm that Izna had given to her tone.

This was a big project, and Izna probably should have felt honored to be considered. The job was an obvious stepping stone to bigger things—perhaps even Andre Glick's office, whenever he was done with it. It was exactly the kind of job that until this moment she would have said she wanted—or at least the kind of job she had expected to take in order to move up the chain. But it felt wrong now. It felt overwhelmingly oppressive. It was a soul-sucking beast of a project that would steal everything she was willing to give it until it was done, and it wasn't really in her field.

"Why me? Why not a military officer—or at least a law enforcement steward?"

Jimison hesitated.

"Andre and I spoke about this for some time," she said. "We both think that people will respond to a civilian leader better than one who wears a uniform."

Izna realized then that Jimison's hesitation had been her tell, her way of gearing up for a lie. The problem now was that Izna didn't understand the reason for the lie, but that Andre was grinning at her like a proud papa, and Jimison was sitting up in her seat, waiting for a response.

Izna was suddenly deeply uncomfortable.

She became intensely aware that the only way out of the room was the doorway across from her desk, and that to get there she would have to go through her visitors. She was tired, and her brain wasn't working like she wanted it to. It was all very disconcerting.

"I see," she said, sitting back with the best smile she could muster. "Can I have a day to consider it?"

"Of course," Jimison said, glancing at Andre.

"Certainly," the director said. "You've had a lot on your plate recently. It's probably best that you take the day and talk it over with your friends. I'm sure you'll come to the right conclusion."

She thanked them both.

When they left she shut her door, returned to her chair, and lay her head on her desk. It was quiet here. The room was cool. She hadn't planned on sleeping, but she was so tired. It felt good to just shut her eyes.

She dreamed then.

Selma was blue, glimmering with chrome flares and dark swirls that floated around her head like hair. Her eyes were star-like, and her smile gave her an edgy sense of calm.

Izna smelled salt water on the breeze, and remembered her week in Jamaica. There was sand between her toes. A canvas roof flapped in the breeze over a hammock, and she saw herself on a sailboard out on the surf and then on a panel speaking at a conference and then driving at breakneck speed over a beach in an airpod with Bethel beside her.

And someone else, too, was there. Right beside her.

They were laughing and screaming to each other with glee.

She wore a violet and white scarf wrapped around her neck that trailed in the wind behind her. She smelled sandalwood ground into the fabric of that scarf. There was a bump, and the scarf unwrapped, then flew backward in the wind, fading away, drifting out over the water on the hot breeze. Izna saw herself reach out, her hand as blue like Selma's, extending as it stretched past her normal reach, stretching to infinity as she grasped the end of the scarf.

She pulled on it, and the scarf snapped back.

Izna woke with a start.

She sat bolt upright and was surprised to see it was past 1800 hours.

A coldness washed over her.

Yes.

The equations were right. It had been there all the time, hidden in plain sight.

She needed to get to the models and the tapes. It would probably take all night, but thanks to her nap she felt refreshed.

She got up and went first to the security lab.

* * *

Twelve standard hours later, Izna Keyes stepped into the Entanglement Lab, happy to see Captain Jimison and Director Glick were already there as well as Detective Marquis and several of his officers. She felt energized. She felt in command, like nothing she had ever felt before. It was like walking on a tightrope, balancing there above a pit of vipers for all to see. She swore she saw a bluish hue across the shell of EC-1.

"Good morning, Ms. Keyes," the captain said. "I was surprised by your message, but I hope you have good news for me."

"I hope I do, too, Captain."

"Isn't this a bit melodramatic, Izna?" Andre said. He glanced around the lab, obviously more than a bit uncomfortable. "You could have just come to the office."

Izna smirked. She reveled in the atmosphere. It felt like being in an old Agatha Christie play.

"I wanted to speak to you here," she said, "because I want Selma to hear me better."

Andre's face darkened. "What in hell do you mean?"

"I've finished my work on her accident," Izna said. "I can now tell you exactly what happened to her."

One of the techs in the audience gasped.

"I warned you," Andre said. "Detective Marquez, please escort Ms. Keyes out of the lab. I am removing her from her position."

"Let her finish, Andre," Jimison said, raising her hand. "I want to hear what she's got to say."

Andre Glick's gaze skipped across the room with the laser-like precision of a caged rat.

She took a step to stand before Andre.

"You convinced the captain to offer me that job as a way to get me out of the tech labs. It was a no-lose situation for you. If I succeeded you would get the credit, and if I failed I would be off the station and out of your hair forever. But either way, a self-contained data engineering project like that would have absorbed my time for the next five years at least."

"You're out of your mind," Andre said. Blood rose to his cheeks.

The captain's expression alone was enough to tell Izna she had been right about Andre's arm-twisting.

"You said this was about Selma," Jimison said when she finally turned her gaze Izna's direction.

"Yes, Captain Jimison. It is."

"Get on with it, then."

"Selma's death was no accident."

"Jesus H. Christ!" Andre said. "How much more of this are we going to have to take?"

"Andre," the captain said firmly.

The room became deathly silent.

"We've been through the math time and time again," Izna said. "And Andre is right. There's nothing there to explain why a premature snap-back happened."

Andre Glick took a sharp breath, but did not say anything.

"But we've been examining the problem from the outside in when we should have been looking at it from the inside out."

"I don't understand," the captain said.

"The math is all correct," Izna replied. "Nothing in the environment she was traveling in could have caused that premature snap-back, not the ship, not the sector she was in, not the connection. All of that is true. There is nothing in the environment that we've looked at that could cause the snap-back. But we're not taking into account the idea that Selma herself might have initiated the event."

"Are you crazy?" Andre burst out again, his face as red as a tomato. "Are you suggesting Selma committed suicide?"

Izna actually laughed then.

"No, Andre. You're the one who must be joking. Selma would never have destroyed herself."

"Then what are you saying? Pilot error?"

Izna walked to EC-1, and ran her hand alongside the gunmetal container. Selma stepped forward then, the part of her that was left, anyway. She stood in silence beside the chamber, draped in blue light, one arm extended toward Izna, and an expression of certainty on her face.

"I'm saying you killed her, Andre. I'm saying you murdered Selma Distofani in cold blood. And I'm saying I've got the models and the background data to prove it."

* * *

Andre Glick was arrested, tried, and eventually sentenced to life in constraint. The truth was that he had been jealous of Selma. He had never really had to play second to anyone before Selma, and Selma was not one to take a back seat for ego's sake. They had broken up the night before the mission. Andre was going to be nothing more than a footnote in history while Selma Distofani would rise to even greater heights.

His background was in data and security systems.

He had not found it hard to adjust the station security systems, and once the monitor data had been altered, all Andre had to do was wait for the programmed time and relieve the security detail guarding EC-1. The vids that remained behind showed him standing guard, rather than breaking the chamber's seals, and they showed him going into the apoplectic fits one might when a lover is killed.

It did not show Selma's reaction, though.

There was no tracking on her attempt to bring the system home earlier than planned. But the math was clear when you turned the tables and saw it from inside the chamber, and other facts on the movements of Andre Glick made the truth as clear.

Andre broke the seal on Entanglement Chamber-1. Selma tried to pilot the craft into an intermediate snap-back, but the probability curve collapsed too quickly and the connections recoiled through space-time with uncontrolled violence.

Selma Distofani died.

Andre Glick, the bereft lover, flew the follow-on mission and lived happily ever after.

Until now.

* * *

It was late. They were in Bethel's quarters, a room with a welcoming quiet, enjoying their last time together for the foreseeable future. The wine was bold, red, and tasted of plum and cherry. There had been a going-away party for Izna earlier that evening, which she had seen as really just an opportunity to say goodbye to Selma for once and for all. Selma hadn't come out of EC-1 since Andre's arrest despite Izna sitting in the Entanglement Lab several times.

That was fine, though.

She hoped Selma was happy.

If that was possible.

In some fashion, it felt like Selma had released her, that she was now expected to fly for them both.

That part made her happy. It gave her a charter, and it gave her a sense of indebtedness that she still needed to take such a bold step as to resign her post and move away.

Izna missed her, though.

"What are you going to do now?" Bethel asked.

Izna shrugged. Her shuttle planetside would leave the next day.

"I don't know," she said. "I'll see my parents for a few days. Then we'll see. Maybe I'll go see Venus."

"That's just a big ball of poison gas."

Izna sipped wine and gave a smile she felt was almost coy. "It's interesting poison gas, though. Did you know they're studying the effects of pressure and heat on quantum processes there in ways that are really remarkable. There's a guy who thinks we can find simple ways to communicate across universes on planets like that."

"Quantum pressure. Great. You're a daredevil now, eh?"

"Maybe," Izna said. "Maybe I am. You should join me."

Bethel shook her head. "That's not my gig, girl. But maybe when you're done world-hopping you'll come back, eh?"

"That would be great."

"Until then, I'll live vicariously through you."

Bethel reached behind the couch and pulled out a box wrapped in paper. "I got you a present," she said.

"You didn't have to do that."

"I know. But I was shopping and it just felt right."

Izna set her wineglass down and tore into the paper. She slipped open the box to reveal a gauzy white scarf with a faint violet and blue pattern woven through it. She recognized it in an instant. It was the scarf of her dream.

"How did you know?" she said as she pulled it from the box.

"Know what?" Bethel replied.

Bethel's expression told Izna that she was telling the truth and had merely picked out something on a whim that she thought might look good.

Izna held it with the fingertips of both hands. It felt as beautiful as it looked. Then she brought it to her nose and inhaled.

The scarf smelled of sandalwood.

"I love it," she said, looking at her friend. "It's perfect."

Ron's Afterword

Turns out I have an obstinate streak.

I sat down specifically to write a ghost story. That was the charter, of course. The opening line tells you that. But in doing that, I decided to challenge myself. Could I write a ghost story in the genre of hard science? That would be difficult, of course, because hard, peer-reviewed science does not exist for such things as ghosts. So, I knew I would have to stick the landing someplace.

It turned into a mystery/detective piece in space, too. Which was fun. What I remember most about writing it was the character of Izna, and the mechanics I went through to lay out the story through her viewpoint. There is, after all, a lot going on here. So much that at various points I've considered expanding and then following her story into a longer work.

We'll see if that happens or not.

Regardless, one can look at the existence of "The Blue Lady of Entanglement Chamber 1" as a representation of my desires to mix and match genres at times. I find that fun.

The next piece is another example of that.

Kagari

ANALOG JANUARY/FEBRUARY 2024

A fiery bolt streaked across the nighttime sky.

Orange fire grew over the western horizon.

Some of the common-bred claimed it was an omen from sky gods. Others held steadfast to the thought that it was a portent of war—a claim considerably more difficult to deny in these times of turmoil. To avoid panic, Father commissioned the scouting expedition that found strange wreckage of twisted metal amid the charred woods, and creatures scattered about, their bodies bloodied and broken.

Only one remained alive.

* * *

The thin feathers above my father's brow arched with anticipation. "Happy birthday, Rythane," he said, gesturing grandly for the sake of all Arroth. "Today you become *prueaxe*."

His words weighed like water in my wings.

His golden teeth, honed for the hunt, gleamed sharp in the brilliant light of Aerthau's Hall, the ceremonial chamber where three centuries prior the great one himself was crowned. Father's subjects filled the sitting area, perched in masses along the walls. Whereas prior to the proceeding they had preened and squawked among themselves, now the trilling of their response to Father's presentation echoed under the domed ceiling despite the expanse of wide gaps to open air at each end.

Their bodies warmed the morning chill.

When the echoes died, they gazed upon me with a crushing mixture of curiosity, devotion, expectation and judgment.

Perched beside him, I placed my arm on the rest of my Father's throne, which was carved of pure crystal and mounted on a spire of granite that rose naturally from the floor. Cloud-fine silk trimmed my provincial blue robe. My wings, folded down my back and sides, curled over my knees in the form appropriate for royalty. A diadem inlaid with aquamarine encircled my head.

Mother sat forward in the balcony.

She performed the role of *kalla* in traditional style, keeping her everyday profile low but showing proper support for the Aerithane.

The age of *prueaxe* is twenty cycles.

It is when a young male in the royal line takes his rightful place at the hand of his father. Although members of common Arroth had followed my life, this was my first public role before them—my first brush with ceremonial function. As fitting, the Hythean choir, resplendent in swathes of crimson, were positioned to my left. An orator read from the speaking perch, telling the events of my life. I found it embarrassing to hear them blown beyond proportion, but the script called for a hero's tale, and they had only me to work with.

I am not my father.

I would be better placed as a common-bred, a follower of natural law rather than its interpreter. Father has explained that this feeling was to be expected, that he had felt similarly in his flights as *prueaxe* and that his father had also before him felt so diminished. I wish I could believe this.

I scanned the crowd, hoping to see Seri among them but unable to discern her.

"And now, my son," Father said in his booming voice. "My *prueaxe*. I present you a token of my pride and love." He took to the air with stately grace, his ceremonial koska swirling about him like a swath of high sky.

Reed players blew their instruments and a choir of voices rose in a single, piercing note.

Activity erupted from the entryway, and the crowd's voice rose in a tumultuous rumble. Six bearers flew forward, laboring under the weight of a waist-high box, and draped fully in golden cloth that hung in the open air like moss from summer trees. They carried it on three sturdy crossbeams that had been threaded through open bores at the top of the box. Arriving, the gift bearers placed the box carefully, if not with an awkward lurch at the end, on the open dais in the center of the Hall.

I stood upright on my perch, letting my feet clench and relax again, feeling talons extend and retract as they removed the crossbeams and left the box. The motion made me wish I were soaring. Made me wish I were on the upper currents alone. Or, no, not alone.

My gaze scanned for Seri once again, and once again came up empty.

Alone then, and with the levers having been removed, I stretched my wings and glided in a rounded path to sand before my Father's present.

The cloth that covered the crate was thin fiber with gold thread.

I slipped it off to reveal a cage.

The audience gasped.

A small, featherless creature huddled in one corner, its legs curled against its chest. It had hair like streak lightning, barren skin of smooth bearing, and wore clothes the color of deep ocean.

I recognized it at once—the creature from the fire.

My father's voice echoed in the chamber. "To you, my son, I present this creature. It is one of a kind, as are you."

The audience applauded.

I bent to examine my gift. It was proportioned similarly to an Arroth, but half my height and without wings. It appeared to be male and, like myself, had arms and legs. Its eyes were round and blue, its nose blunt. Its feet were flat rather than curled and useful.

I looked at my father, then scanned the audience as they still applauded, seeing then the true purpose of the gift.

By presenting the creature in this fashion, Father had reduced its status from that of a wild avatar of the Sky Gods to one of a simple pet the *prueaxe* was expected to keep. In one stroke, he had quelled the fear that had spread like gale-blown fire through the ranks of the common-bred.

The creature stood, filling the box's height. Its talonless hands gripped the bars. Its eyes were deep with anger, and it trembled in terror as it called out in a ragged voice. Even though its language was arcane, these were expressions I understood. It was in a place where it didn't belong, and in a situation that it didn't understand.

I, however, did understand.

"Thank you, Father. I will keep it sound. I will protect it, shelter it from torrents when the storms come and see that it enjoys open skies."

The audience smiled.

My father nodded.

* * *

I named the creature Kagari after the animals that forage on the ground. He reminded me of them, except that his hair was neither as thick nor as prevalent. Like the kagari, his hands had fingers and thumbs, but no hunting talons. And like the kagari, his teeth were flat.

I fed him kagari food, and he ate it.

The name seemed to fit.

The bearers took Kagari to my aerie, where, despite the fact that I let him have free run, he merely sat quietly against the wall, eating sparely and staring out the window with a vacant expression.

He tried to run away the first night, but the manor proper is suspended from the tallest cliffs of Arroth, and Kagari had no wings. I found him in the morning on the window ledge, clinging to the wall, his body quivering, his fingers pale with fatigue.

* * *

That morning I ate with my father in his pod.

Unlike his public chambers, Father's private aerie—which was positioned near the peak of the tallest mountain in the South Ranges—was decorated in simple fashion.

We perched at a bare wooden plank and ate from ceramic plates. The morning skies were calm, so the pod was left open to expose the arc of the horizon, dusty in the distant view. The morning sun slanted across the platform, bathing the cliffside of the aerie with soft orange light. The scents of rock and harsh foliage joined that of the food.

To Father's routine, our meal started with hard nuts and a jelly imported from the lowlands. We drank clear water from goblets and finished with flesh from pulled from jonga and kayala.

I am an only child, and with my ascension to *prueaxe* my father now had an heir. Already, lines of anxiety had lifted from his expression.

"A *prueaxe* needs a mate, Rythane," he said. "I believe Cyleen of Jaeron is the most appropriate choice."

I considered my response.

Cyleen was beautiful. Her family held sky along the north ridges of the Crystal Mountains. Their air was clear and smooth, and their land full of livestock. Their blood ran with strong leaders, too. Perhaps of greater import, an alliance with Jaeron would make both the Parchech to our south and the Evvarian to our east take note. Both had advanced against us over the past cycle, and both were suffering drought this spring that foretold of difficulties they might face in feeding their populations in the wintertime to come.

All this made Cyleen an obvious choice.

"Perhaps," I replied, speaking words I had practiced several times. "Arroth might be made stronger if I were to pair from within."

My father frowned. "Provide me your reasoning."

"If war is on the horizon, the resolve of common Arroth would be strengthened if they were ruled by those who were true-bred."

It was not an argument I liked, but it was one he would consider.

Father sat in silence.

"Jaeron could still be made an ally through treaty," I added. "We share a border, and our common cause could be enough to bind us."

"I see," Father said. "And I suppose Seri would be a stronger match for the good of all Arroth?"

"She would make a strong *kalla*."

"Seri is common-bred, Rythane. As much as I like her, you know she cannot be brought into the house."

There it was.

Common-bred meant incapable, unimportant. Common-bred cannot go to school or have sway in decisions of rulers. Common-bred have no skill but that of their family trade. It is the law, the natural order of Arroth and all other of Aerthau.

"She's different, Father," I said.

"How long has our family ruled Arroth?" my father replied.

"Over three centuries."

"You doubt three centuries of history?"

"I only know what I see."

Father grinned. "That is good. That skill will make you a fine ruler someday, Rythane. But now you are young. You still have need to grow, to see reason in our ways. When you are older you will see why these orders have given us three centuries of peace."

I nodded.

Still, I felt sick. My father would arrange this match as his own father had arranged his pairing to my mother and his father's father had arranged before him.

"I understand," I said.

"I will call for a council with Taggach today."

* * *

I met Seri for the last time that evening.

We sat on the sundown side of the canyon, resting our backs against the red cliffs as nighttime crept across the sky. The swirling wind came from the north. Seri clutched her thin knees to her chest. Our arms brushed, and stray feathers clung to one another.

Seri turned to me, her gaze like hot metal, telling me she knew what I needed to say.

"My father is to meet with Taggach of Jaeron," I said.

She waited, eyes glittering in the growing darkness, but it was all I could manage.

"You are *prueaxe*. It was bound to happen." She stood, then bent to kiss my cheek. "Have a good life, Rythane. Rule well."

Her wings caught thick wind, and I watched as she glided over the canyon and turned toward her home.

I sat alone for several minutes, her kiss burning against my cheek.

The stone drew heat from my back.

My jaw clenched. I swallowed what felt like a handful of pebbles.

Seri had been the strong one, as always. She had taken the conversation from me, knowing what needed to be done and closing our relationship as it needed to be closed.

She would make a better *prueaxe* than me.

The sky had grown to indigo. I spread my wings and stepped into the wind.

* * *

I began talking to Kagari that night.

The sun had fully set, and the western sky was the color of a cut sapphire.

The evening stars, Hevron and Ravell, blazed to the north, and a chill breeze swirled through my aerie. Below, in the lower reaches of the foothills, the common-bread prepared for the evening in the tree hutches and cavern openings. Far away, a messenger was likely arriving a the House of Taggach of Jaeron.

I pulled a blanket over my shoulders and thought of the future.

Who would Cyleen be? Would she laugh at my humor? Would her eyes glisten when I arrived in her sight?

Would she be interested in learning from me?

In other words, would she be like Seri?

Doubtful. Impossible, actually.

Kagari huddled under a blanket. His hair was as tousled as a common hawk's nest. His eyes were haggard, and his cheeks chalky.

"You are not eating," I said to Kagari.

Kagari did not indicate he heard me.

"Do not die on me."

I knew he could not understand, but the sound of my voice echoing in open space was somehow comforting. Speaking aloud released unseen pressure and gave my thoughts a place to grow.

So I told Kagari about Seri, lingering over our first meeting and how we had flown to where the air was thin and ice seemed to form around our eyes; how the warmth of her excitement felt like sitting in the sunshine. I explained how I would meet her after lessons to discuss what I had learned. I chuckled as I remembered her first questions, then grew serious when I told Kagari how I realized I was breaking code.

Common-bred are not to be taught the great truths of the world.

The law is very clear on that point.

Yet, Seri had no difficulty understanding me. She listened intently and even questioned specific points she hadn't followed, leading me to new perspectives of my own. It was that inquisitiveness that changed me. Her ability to find the right questions that gave me the presence to see the truth of her existence.

Seri, I knew in my heart, would outdo me in any classroom.

When I was finished telling my stories, I paused and spent time glazing out the window into the star-strewn sky.

Kagari looked at me then, cocking his head.

The muscles around his eyes constricted, drawing together and making his focus more intense. He stood before me, his head at the level of my waist.

"Stewart," he said, clenching his fist to his chest.

I was speechless.

"Stewart." He repeated both the word and the motion.

I did my best to mouth the foreign sound, and Kagari smiled, his dull, white teeth showing in the dim light of my aerie.

"Rythane," I said, pointing a taloned finger at my own chest, still disbelieving what was happening.

"Rythane," Stewart mimicked. His voice was flat and carried none of the inflection an Arroth's would. But the word was recognizable.

I smiled at him.

We spent the rest of the night pointing and listing off names. I thrilled as I learned pieces of his language. Honnea was "moon"; creatha was "bed" or maybe "nest". We covered "floor" and "window" and "air" and several others. Though he could not make hard sounds, I had greater difficulty speaking his language than Stewart had speaking Arroth. Both of us rushed through the room picking items and naming them, exchanging hurried glances before racing to the next item. By the time Honnea hit its apex, we had covered most of the aerie.

We were exhausted, too.

Stewart retreated to his blanket. I lay in my "bed" and stared at him, my troubles temporarily forgotten. He had language. He was no mere animal, not a pet to be simply kept—as were the kagari I had named him after.

"Goodnight," he said as he pulled a blanket over his shoulder.

Uncertain of what he meant, I remained silent.

Stewart soon made his sleeping sounds.

I watched his chest rise and fall as Honnea slipped toward the horizon.

* * *

A *prueaxe* has little to do but watch and learn—but there is more of that than can be imagined. Politics, ceremony, etiquette, history. They all touch the life of a *prueaxe* in ways that influence every moment of every day.

I watched the way our people treated my father, how they bowed with his approach, how they provided ideas and interpretations of events but deferred to his opinion in the end. My father was a strong leader, bold and decisive. He weighed advice with a measured hand and made his decisions justly. He allowed discussion until the conversation became circular, then he chose a path.

In this process, I saw his interpretations and the reason for his decisions.

I saw that not all issues are as clear-cut as they first appear, that behavior is learned and that generations of such lessons have made the Arroth expect to be told what to do.

The Aerithane cannot afford to be seen as weak lest his people lose their ability to overcome obstacles of life.

For several lightsets I did nothing but watch and learn how my people are led.

Each evening I returned to my aerie and shared words with Stewart. We both learned how to speak with each other rapidly enough, but nuances of each language were still mysterious.

I did not tell my father of Stewart's language because, as much as I would have coveted his counsel on the matter, I also feared that Father may see Stewart as an affront to the Arroth. If common-bred were not to be educated, a pet would clearly cause similar controversy.

So, to some practical degree, I kept Stewart's language to myself to ensure his safety.

Yet, I had to admit there was something else that restrained my disclosure.

A secret is, in some fashion, power.

And the secret of Stewart's language was, perhaps, the only power I actually held.

\#

Taggach replied to Father's offer in proper time, sending word that he would bring Cyleen to Arroth. They would arrive in ten lightsets.

I went to my creatha late that evening.

Despite pleasant temperature and a wind that blew soothing tones against the manor walls, I was still unable to sleep.

"My life is changing, Stewart," I said, not certain he would understand.

Stewart sat up in his creatha, his form looming like an apparition in Honea's weak light. "What's wrong?"

I sighed. "I am *prueaxe*, now. I am to pair."

Stewart hesitated. "Seri?"

I shook my head. "No." The image of Seri's face hung in my mind.

"Why no?" Stewart replied. His use of broken language mimicked his understanding of Arroth politics.

"I cannot."

Again: "Why?"

I sat up, letting blankets fall around me. The chill air prickled across my skin and made me restless.

"It is not done."

"Arroth no ..." Stewart let the sentence dangle as he struggled over a word. Our shared vocabulary was functional more than ideological. With the air of inspiration, he went to the window. Pointing outside, he spoke a word in his own language. "Free?"

I mimicked the word, but did not understand.

"Free," Stewart repeated. "Fly." He made a symbol of flapping wings. "Free."

"Arroth flies anywhere he wants," I replied.

He looked into space again, obviously still struggling with concepts and language. He flapped his arms and said, "Fly to Seri?"

I laughed at this. Fly to Seri. "No," I said.

"No free, then."

"No," I replied. "I am not free in that manner."

Stewart's face grew rigid. His lips turned downward, and his eyes grew hooded. "Like Stewart."

I felt sorry for him then and ashamed of myself.

I watched him for some time, worry building like gray clouds. His eyes were shrunken and growing dark. I had found gouges and scratches at the door over the past few lightsets, but had ignored them to the best of my ability. But the fact of his raw fingers and hands made certain assessments obvious.

Someday perhaps I could bring Stewart into the world, to expose him to situations and let him learn to live among common-bred. But now he was a prisoner, a play toy as my father had once called him.

"It is just not done, Stewart," I finally replied. "Seri is common-bred. She is not fit to be *kalla*."

"You love her," Stewart said.

I nodded. "I think so. But even if a royal could consider a common-bred, my father would still choose Cyleen." I glanced to the south where even imagining the Parchech gathering their forces made the feathers surrounding my neck tingle. "War could be on the horizon," I said. "She is the best choice."

"What if Rythane flies to Seri anyway?"

"It will not happen."

"What if?"

I thought. What if I did leave with Seri? Such things occurred in common circles but, in all of history no *prueaxe* or Aerithane had ever made such a bold flight. The scandal would be devastating.

The thought was ice along my spine.

"No, Stewart," I replied. "I could not do that."

"Because Seri is common-bred?"

"Yes." My reply left my mouth dry.

He was quiet, staring out the window. "Our common-bred gave my people the stars," he finally said.

I slipped under my blankets and lay in the darkness, trying to ignore him and go to sleep. Tomorrow would be a long day.

Stewart walked to my creatha and stood over me. His stare penetrated like invisible talons. "How can you lead with your heart," he said, "if you cannot follow it?"

Then he returned to his creatha.

Wind whistled outside, and the sound of Stewart's breathing eventually rasped in the air.

I did not sleep for a long time.

* * *

My father met Taggach's caravan in Aerthau's Hall. I felt eyes upon me as I waited, but I did not react. I was *prueaxe*, after all. I understood my position.

The reception was exquisite, complete with fresh field hare and seared bloodsauce.

A carafe of spring water was placed at each table in cool decanters that sweated despite the Hall's altitude. After the welcoming ritual, my father and Taggach led the procession to the Common Hall. Taggach's sash was the soft blue of midday sky, Father's the color of night surrounding Honnea. I followed in their wakes, pleased that I was able to remain stoic, if not calm.

We took our places, father and Taggach in the center of the main perch, me to my father's left. In the *kalla*'s alcove, Mother was radiant in shimmering aquamarine, her freshly preened wings crossed before her in perfect form.

Seri stood in the back of the chamber.

Our gazes locked.

The feathers along her brow turned downward, and her shoulders slumped with the weight of avoided inevitability. As strong as she was, Seri had not actually come to grips with our parting.

115

I dragged my gaze from her.

What did she think of me? I did not ask to be born a *prueaxe*. Did she hold me responsible for my position?

Deep inside though, I was pleased to know Seri ached for me as much as I ached for her.

Horns blew, and the chamber grew instantly still.

Father's royal guard opened doors at the far end of the hall, and music began.

More of the guard escorted Cyleen in, flying her perch through the doorway, then pausing as she collected herself.

She was tall and regal. Her angular face reminded me of my mother's. She took wing and glided down the central corridor with controlled grace, using the rising warmth of torchlight to glide so elegantly above. The audience whispered softly as she landed before me, her ceremonial garb of cinnamon colors settling gently around her. Her eyes were raised to meet mine rather than downcast as was traditional.

I smiled.

She would be a modern *kalla*. I could not help but admire her.

"Welcome, Cyleen of Jaeron," I said. "I have eagerly awaited your arrival, yet your presence has still stolen my breath."

Cyleen returned my smile, a dimple forming in the soft feathers of her left cheek. "I am pleased to be here, Rythane of Arroth. You, too, have taken my breath."

My father and his guest beamed with happy splendor. Tears glittered in my mother's eyes. In the distance, Seri slipped silently from the meeting chamber.

* * *

I had dinner with my father that night.

Cyleen and I would formally pair the following afternoon.

"You are quiet," my father said.

I nodded.

"I am sure you have much to think about."

Again, I nodded. My father's stare was piercing. I wanted to talk to him, but my heart ground against my ribs, thudding with the precision of a death dive.

"I have decided my first task as *prueaxe*," I said.

Father grinned. "I knew you would, son. What will it be?"

"I want to build schools for common-bred."

"I see," Father said, a red anger rising to his cheeks. "Despite law that forbids it, you intend to attempt to educate the lesser Arroth?"

"There are good minds in the common-bred ranks, Father," I said. "I've seen them. Seri, for one, is brilliant."

I waited for a response, and when none came, I filled the silence.

"It is a practical matter, Father. If we use all our resources, we will be stronger than the Parchech to the south. Stronger, also, than the Evvarian to the East."

Father's brows knitted, and he stared at me until his long silence became unbearable.

My face flushed with embarrassed heat. "It was just a thought, Father."

"It was an inappropriate thought. The Arroth live in balance now. It is a balance that has provided prosperity for centuries, yet now you intend to break it?"

Anything I said would merely add to father's anger.

"Who put this idea into your head?"

"No one, Father," I said, panic flickering along my spine.

"I have raised you to be *prueaxe*, Rythane. These thoughts are not yours. Was it Seri? Has she poisoned your ideals?"

My stomach tightened. He would have Seri dismissed from the community without second thought if I did not offer another culprit. It was a thought I could not bear.

"No, Father. It was Stewart," I said, giving voice to something that was not quite a total lie.

"Stewart?" My answer took him aback. "Who is Stewart?"

"Your gift, Father."

"You mean Kagari?"

"I was wrong to give him that name. He explained he is Stewart."

Father waved an annoyed hand. "Whatever its name, you can't expect me to believe Kagari can voice such thoughts."

"He is intelligent, Father. He has language."

Father swallowed his food with no little anger, then called to his servant. The young Arroth scurried over, bowing with wingtips lowered in proper respect. The feathers around his eyes were yellow, and he wore a simple robe.

"Go to my son's aerie. Bring the pet."

The servant left with a nod.

Father strode to the window and stretched his wings, looking as if he were going to fly away. The position of Aerithane is fraught with difficulties. It would be good for him to get more time in the currents.

I cleared my throat. "There are rumors of the Parchech building an army."

"The Parchech can always be trusted to build armies," he replied.

The servant returned shortly with Stewart in tow, then bowed quietly and took our dirty plates with him as he left.

"Stewart," I said, rising.

"Rythane," he replied. His expression showed caution tinged with fear.

Despite our earlier conversation, my father stared slack-jawed.

"He knows a trick."

"There is more." I plucked a single feather from my back. "Feather," I said.

Stewart smiled. "Hathee," he replied with the proper term. We continued with "foot" and "eyes" and "table."

Father stared at Stewart. His wings flickered with interest. "I'll be," he said. "You have been *prueaxe* for only a short while and already you are performing miracles."

I started to explain that this was as much Stewart's doing as mine, but the glimmer in my father's eye made me realize it would be like speaking to the wind.

"And you say it was Kagari who framed you first attempt at policy?"

I nodded. "It was."

"I see," Father said, one taloned finger scratching absently against the tabletop. His brows knit together. "Go to the kitchen and give the women thanks for a meal well served. Then go to your aerie. You are dismissed."

Knowing better than to argue, I stood and left.

* * *

The pairing was everything a royal event should be.

I stood alone on the bonding perch, covered in robes of rich blue. The royal ring of Arroth glittered from my finger, and a silver medallion hung from my neck to nestle in the soft feathers at my breast.

Families from every territory attended, including the Parchech and the Evvarian.

A falconer performed midair feats, and blue-feathered dancers did the traditional fertility tribute to Aerthau and Sabine. My father and mother sat together on this occasion, Mother to his right, one hand placed with appropriate precision under his.

Music rose and Cyleen entered.

Her multi-layered robes were sheer. A belt of eagle feathers twined around her thin waist, reaching midway up her torso. Her feathers shone with preparation. A silver necklace matching mine hung from her neck.

The procession was achingly slow.

The choir sang, voices twisting in the air like swallows in their mating dance.

The audience stared at Cyleen as she flew around the entirety of the Hall, her beauty and the powerful meaning of the moment overwhelming them. Several minutes later, she joined me. I took her hand and quoted passage.

She replied as required.

I gazed into her eyes and saw nothing.

Her gaze held no love or warmth. Nor did it hold fear or anger or animosity. How could it? Cyleen, too, was performing her duty. Just as her mother had, and hers before her.

I pulled the amulet from around my neck as she removed hers. I placed mine over her head, settling it properly in place. She returned the act.

I took to the air and led Cyleen in the pairing dance. The dance of young love.

Together, we flew a slow circle around the chamber, her hand cool but firm in mine, talons clasped, adjacent wings pressed together into a single streamlined rudder. The audience applauded and shouted encouragement. We nodded curtly, accepting their good wishes.

The circuit complete, I led her to the hall's entrance.

We flew away from the manor, away from the cliffs.

Arriving at the caverns, we rose on a warm draft, twisting about each other, our robes a mesh of blue and white that twined into a single unit. We rose, two pairs of wings beating the air until it grew thin and cold.

At the apex, I stared at Cyleen and felt our distance. Our lips met.

She was soft and supple, tasting of fresh current. But her kiss was perfunctory, as, I assume she would have judged mine. Our wings stopped. And, still locked in the kiss, we plummeted.

Wind whistled. Feathers ruffled against the fall.

At first, the ground seemed far distant. Then it rushed closer and closer, faster and faster.

Still we remained locked.

Our robes tangled, beating against the air with resonant thumps. At the last moment, we split, Cyleen turning toward the manor, me gliding out over the land of my father.

It was done.

We were paired.

* * *

Cyleen and I made our creatha that evening in the *prueaxe* chamber my father had newly designated. My responsibilities kept me occupied all the next day. This means I did not discover what Father had done until I returned to my prior aerie the following night.

The room was silent.

Stewart's bed was undisturbed.

He was not gazing forlornly out the window, nor was he nibbling at the kagari fruits that had become his favorite food.

His absence told me what I needed to know.

Father would not kill him, of course.

Instead, Stewart would be taken far away and released to the wild. I would never see him again. Perhaps he would be happier with his freedom, but common sense said Stewart could not survive either the creatures or the diseases he would encounter in the wild.

My stomach filled with rocks.

Outside, the setting sun spread fantail rays over the darkening sky.

I felt small. Powerless.

Unable to turn against the wind.

But I felt something else, too. Something that might have been anger, except that it was deeper than that. Different.

My father was wrong, I realized. The truth of this burned with power I had never felt before. My father was wrong about the common-bred. He was wrong about Stewart. My father was wrong, and it would undoubtedly cost Stewart his life.

Unless.

I went to the window and scanned the sky.

"I am sorry," I said to no one.

I stepped outside the ledge and looked at the ground below that Stewart had so often stared at with such longing. It spread into a black horizon, lined with trees and grassy patches and the fields where the common-bred grew jonga and payal root. The smell of its soil rode the wind. Where would father have commanded Stewart be released? I didn't know, but the chill of the night against my chest did nothing to cool the heat rising in my cheeks.

I set my jaw, and perhaps for the first time stepped into the wind with a firm purpose in my heart.

I flew east first, then over spans of rocks and ledges of mountain country that guarded our northern border. I flew with great speed, my wings ripping the current rather than working with it. It made my blood burn hotter.

I dove with great abandon through dark sky to examine trails and treemark.

I became hungry, but still I pressed on into the darkness.

I grew tired, but my mission ached deeply, and I could no more stop now than I could keep current from flowing.

To the west owls soared over treetops.

In the trees, kagari families nested in slings.

I saw buck deer drink from the river running clean and pure down the mountainside.

A pack of han prowled a stretch of the wilderness far to the south.

Yet of Stewart, I saw nothing.

As I drew closer to the city, I hovered over common-bred villages. I saw their fields and ranches. I soared against the wind and examined closely the farm where I knew Seri's family dwelled, their aerie built firmly in the crook of a great redwood. The lands here were well-tended and appeared more prosperous than those of her neighbors. Heat signatures of their crop foraged in the foliage.

A thought of Cyleen came to me, then.

She had done nothing wrong.

What would she feel if she knew I was soaring over this common-bred field?

I turned away, trading altitude for speed and thinking about many things I had seen this evening, for I *had* seen many things, and, in some ways, I had seen those things for the first time.

I did not, however, see Stewart. Nor did I find any indication of his eventual demise.

I returned to my old aerie as the sun was rising.

I sat on the ledge where Stewart had spent so many mornings, and remembered how first light used to touch the white streak of his hair and make it appear as if it were aflame. I was tired to my bones.

My anger had faded but not fallen fully away. It was instead changed, had undergone a metamorphosis into firm resolution. My muscles ached from the evening's exercise, and my head was filled with ideas that would not settle. But I knew one thing for certain.

It was time for me to soar my own path.

* * *

When I arrived at our chamber, I found Cyleen sitting in the eastern sun. Her maiden was weaving silver thread through the coarse feathers of her forewing.

I stood in the doorway amid an awkward silence.

"You should go," she said to her maiden.

"I'm sorry to have left you," I said when we were alone.

"There is no harm. No one is aware my creatha was empty last night." Her eyes were wide as she looked up at me. "Where did you go?"

I sat next to her.

"I fear you have paired poorly," I said.

"That may be, but I will judge that for myself. Will you answer my question?"

"I was looking for someone."

"Seri?"

I was taken aback by the directness of her accusation.

"Did you think Jaeron's intelligence so poor that I was unaware of your feelings for her?"

"No," I said. "I admit I soared across her family aerie at one point last evening, but it was not my destination."

She looked at me as if she was scrying for truth. Apparently, she saw enough there to warrant further conversation.

"So, what was your destination?"

I told her about Stewart.

Cyleen was a kind listener, and the words flowed more easily than I expected.

I told her of our conversations, and about my failed decision to build schools. I confessed to blaming Stewart for the root of the idea when it had been completely mine. And I finished by revealing what my father had done in response.

"You were looking for him?" she said.

"Yes."

"And did you find him?"

I shook my head and rubbed my fingers over tired eyes.

She put a warm hand on my knee.

I looked at her.

She crossed her arms over her chest. "I think I have paired well," she said. "Except my mate is not the brightest when it comes to investigation."

"Excuse me?"

"You're thinking too much like your father, and not enough like Stewart."

I furrowed my brow.

"You don't need to know where your father sent Stewart. You need to know only where Stewart would go from that point."

I felt the excitement of light dawning.

"The site of his crash," I said. I stood. "I've got to go."

Cyleen took firm hold of my arm and said a single word.

"No."

"I am *prueaxe*," I said to her. "I will do as I say."

She pulled me to my seat once again.

"You've been in the air all night. I'll not allow my husband to fly without proper nourishment. Go to the creatha and rest. I will order late first-meal for you, and suggest your sleep is due to the extravagance of our ..." her feathers roughened "... activities."

She believed me, I realized. And she understood. I was astounded at her decisiveness and found myself buoyed by the sensation of having a partner.

"When you finish eating," she said, letting her hand slide down my arm and to my hand. "We will take our pairing flight west. It is only proper that your mate would want to see the site of the great fireball."

Our talons entwined.

"I still cannot agree that you have paired well," I said. "But it is clear that I have."

* * *

As always, on-lookers followed us.

The sky was clear, and the sun was harsh as is normal for a summer's mid-day.

As fitting our roles, we smiled and gave perfunctory waves.

Flying with Cyleen on my left made me feel strong. It is not a feeling I was used to, but I knew even then that it was one I would become well acquainted with.

We came upon the wreckage in late afternoon.

A warm vortex filled our wings, and I escorted Cyleen around the perimeter in looping passes so I could point out the path of the fireball. It had first impacted Yandau's ridge, then careened down the valley to destroy a swath of trees and burn darkened patches into wild grasslands that the land was already recovering. Somewhere the wreckage had caught a strange angle and skipped three times before coming to a rest just before the river. Father's expedition had returned with many samples of strange and fantastic materials from the wreckage, but pieces of the craft were still scattered along this path, and the main cabin had remained unmoved.

Cyleen asked a hundred questions, most of which I had no answers for.

After we had circled the area long enough to satisfy our onlookers, I bent a wing, and we flew down to the rocky riverbed. We landed directly across from a large gash that rent the cabin. Mud and grime covered its gray exterior, and riverweed had already grown around one side. A tangled worm-mass of equipment hung from its torn carcass, but I could see past it into the craft.

"It has no wings," Cyleen said. "How did it fly?"

I did not tell her that I had once asked Stewart that very question, nor did I tell her how he had replied.

Instead, I took her hand.

"Come," I said, and walked her to the open gash.

It was not big enough for me to get through, but as we approached I heard a skittering similar to that I had grown accustomed to.

"Stewart?" I called.

I peered into the craft. It was full of debris. A gray panel sat at an angle against the far wall and a reddish-brown stain smeared the floor leading to the space under the panel.

Stewart lay in a pathetic ball, his hair matted, his face bloody and pale. Though the sun had baked the craft, his entire body shook as if he were freezing.

He was hurt.

"Stewart?"

The opening was too small for me to fit into, so I tried to pull it apart. The metallic frame bent, but I could not budge it far enough to get in.

Above us, the onlookers seemed to burst with new energy.

"Help me, Cyleen!"

She pulled at one edge of the craft and I took the other.

The gash opened farther under our effort, but was still too small.

Too small for me.

Cyleen, though, tucked her wings close over her shoulders and stepped through. She went directly to where Stewart lay, then knelt beside him. Stewart pulled away, but had no strength to his movement. His side bled heavily, and the movement took much out of him. She looked over her shoulder, her eyes wide.

"Stewart," I said in his language. "You are ... broken."

He grunted a reply.

"Let Cyleen help you."

His eyes slowly closed, then snapped open. His head faded to one side.

Cyleen did not wait. She lifted him as if he were a child, then handed him to me through the gash.

We raced to the Aerithane's tower as quickly as we could, Stewart in my arms, Cyleen to my left. I was fatigued from so many hours aloft. My wings burned to hold us in the air, but I managed, gazing upon him as we flew. His jaw was slack, and his hair swirled in the current. His skin was dirty, and his fingertips were scarred and stained in brown blood. The wound in his side was fierce and deep.

I took him directly to the infirmary, and we sat outside as the medicine squad worked.

I stood and paced as the long hours and lack of sleep caught up with me.

Finally unable to pace longer, I put my head in my hands, my temples pounding.

"You have done what you could," Cyleen said.

"I could have told father the truth."

"It would not have helped. Your father is like mine, willing to use a convenient mistruth if it serves what he sees as the greater good. He would have found a way to release Stewart sometime."

I knew this was true.

"It would have helped *me*, though." I sat back and closed my eyes, my head against the cool wall.

Cyleen rubbed my knee.

"Then I have truly paired well," she said.

I opened my eyes to see her fingers were stained brown by Stewart's blood, as was my robe.

Excited voices came from down the hall.

Our fathers, the Aerithane's of Arroth and Jaeron, rounded the corner.

"What have you done?" Father said as he came to stand before me.

I stood. Cyleen stood boldly next to me, her shoulder brushing mine and giving me the strength I needed. I felt close to her then. I took her hand and felt the power of her grip.

"I have brought Stewart here."

"Did I not say you have greater duties now?"

"I have no greater duty than the welfare of those under my ward, Father. And you gave me this ward yourself."

Father's eyes tested me.

I set my jaw and held his stare.

Taggach spoke. "How did this creature escape?"

"He has always wanted to be free," I replied, not breaking gaze with my father. "As do all creatures of intelligence. I was too blind to see this, but my father, in his wisdom, gave this creature his desire."

We held positions for another moment, then Father's face relaxed and I saw my message register.

"How is Kagari?" he asked.

"His name is Stewart," I said.

My father put his hand on my shoulder. "Yes, his name is Stewart. I apologize for my error. How is he?"

"We don't know," Cyleen replied.

Father looked at her, shocked that she had spoken in my place, then he saw our intertwined talons and perhaps the determination on our faces.

He shared a glance with Taggach, then nodded and sat on a bench across from us.

We discussed Stewart's condition and I recounted our flight to find him. Father waited for some time, but then his duties pulled him and Taggach away.

The room grew quiet.

"You may leave if you wish," I told Cyleen.

Instead, she asked more questions about Stewart, and about Arroth, and about my feelings toward her home. She listened to me, nodding at times and giving grim smiles at bittersweet moments. She took interest in Stewart's comments about the common-bred and about life in the stars, so we discussed philosophy.

I told her about my flight of last evening, and the sense of commitment I felt as I flew over all of Arroth.

"You will make a fine Aerithane," she said at one point, though I sloughed it off.

When the medicine giver returned, he found us sitting together in the entry arch, her head on my shoulder.

He carried a dark look upon his face.

We had been too late.

* * *

Histories speak of the events that occurred that fall—of Parchech's offensive, and of the bleak Winter War that followed. The stories of the fall of Taggach and the maiming of my father are now well-taught, as are tales of the restoration and the great cultivations of Arroth that saved the land for all.

These histories speak well of me.

That is true.

But I have never wasted an opportunity to give Cyleen her due.

And, of course, Seri also.

It was Seri who had already implemented my plans for common-bred education, and it was her family who taught the four lands to grow and cultivate well. She is the one who worked tirelessly to establish the nutritional labors I commanded, and to explore new ways of supporting our people.

Seri lives with a mate she selected herself.

Her daughter is nearing three cycles and will go to school the next.

She is happy.

Yet, I am the benefactor of histories.

I know this is because I have been Aerithane of the combined territories for ten cycles, now. And I know it is because the Arroth wish to be led, as I suspect most of any intelligence do.

Yet, each change has its own pace.

For example, I grew quickly to love Cyleen with all of my heart, as she has grown to love me. She is beautiful. She is intelligent, and strong. She is a popular *kalla*. I am proud to say I am the first Aerithane to take food in sight of my mate. I remember and still cherish the expression on my servant's face this first occurred, and I remember the scandal it created as news spread among the people of Arroth.

But I also remember how quickly that scandal faded as my practice became norm.

I know some Arroth still find discomfort in this. But they cope. Slowly, they will change, and I believe it is my job to see these changes happen.

Some ask me why I believe this is so.

To them I say, "Look at our land. Is it not better? Have we not stopped the border wars that once savaged our four peoples?"

Still there are doubters.

We do not need more change, these doubters say. We have gone far enough already.

To those I have this final story to impart.

One day, recently, I sat in the western tower with Cyleen and our son, Yerinor, named for his grandfather before him. On this day my son stood tenuously, stretching his wings for balance. He staggered to the window ledge and gazed out across land that stretched to the horizon.

For a moment I recalled a memory of Stewart standing at my aerie window, staring upward, his eyes squinted against the sun. It was a clear morning that day. First light had broken and it blazed in Stewart's hair.

"For one with no wings," I said, "you stare into the sky often."

"They will come," Stewart said.

I chuckled. He had already told me stories of crafts that fly where the sky grows too thin for any Arroth wing to find purchase.

"Your craft had no wings," I said. "How could it fly?"

Stewart puzzled over my words.

I flapped my wings. "No fly," I said in his language, and pointed at him, and then the sky.

He shrugged his shoulders and gave a thin smile before turning his gaze back to search the early morning sky.

"They will come," he said again. "They will come."

So, for those who say we have gone far enough already, I say this.

The world is large.

My father thought we survived best by controlling all things. He thought we grow stronger by restraining change.

I do not hold my father in disregard. But I believe he was wrong in these things.

I believe we are stronger together than we are apart, and I believe we need to understand others because even greater change is always on its way. I learned this from Stewart. I remember his words.

I believe they will come.

When they do, I hope our children will play together.

Ron's Afterword

"Kagari" went through many iterations, and will always be one of my favorite stories simply because at one time Brigid, my daughter (who was quite young at the time), said it was her favorite story. I think she liked Stuart, as I recall. I think she also liked the fact that it comes wrapped in fantasy-flavored tropes, which—due to my genetically ingrained desire to bend genres at times—I did on purpose. Like with "The Blue Lady of Entanglement Chamber 1" before it, which was my attempt to tell a hard SF ghost story, "Kagari" is my effort to make a hard-ish SF fantasy world happen.

I wrote it first as a short story, then expanded it, then contracted it. At one point Stan Schmidt looked at it and suggested I let it sit, then come back at it with a stronger sense of the alien. I did that, but by then Trevor Quachri had taken the *Analog* editor's seat, so I wasn't sure it would … um … fly with him. Luckily, it did.

I still get the urge to come back to Kagari's world.

I think there's a lot more here.

Apparently other folks do, too, because I've received notes from readers suggesting they might like more.

Throw it on the idea pile, right?

Then, again, it was Brigid's favorite story at one time. So maybe it should get priority?

Hillman, Charles Dallas, Age: 35, No Partner, Parents: Deceased

ANALOG MARCH/APRIL 2021

Charles Hillman suddenly found his reasons for agreeing to this experiment lacking. Yes, he was broke, and taking the job got him off the street for a bit. But when you're strapped to a cold examiner's table in a room where the only sound is the cranking up of a power coil, and you're staring down the barrel of a computer-controlled laser gun, these things tend to take a backseat.

The technician scanned a plastic clipboard.

The air was dry, its smell antiseptic.

"Ready, Mr. Hillman?"

Charles glanced at the pointy instrument hovering over him like the claw of a giant praying mantis. "Ready as ever."

The tech stepped behind a shielded wall.

A mechanical whir accompanied the laser's movements.

Rapid-fire clicking ensued.

A light flared.

Then there was pain.

Unexpected pain.

Pain, sharp and bitter and tasting of electricity.

They lied, he thought. *The bastard lied!*

* * *

It all started the evening he spent at Rachel's.

They'd gone to a movie, some Paul Gerard and Alicia Harmon rom-com that satisfied for thirty minutes then faded to nowhere. It was late. They sat on the couch in his high-rise apartment, looking out over the city lights and sipping white wine as she commented on the pen and ink images of buildings and trees around his college campus he'd put on the wall.

"They're yours?" she said when she said she liked them.

"Yeah. I was in art school until I realized it doesn't pay worth a damn."

He'd been pretty good though. He liked that she noticed. That was back in the days before he'd gotten this crappy job that paid well enough to afford this place but now just bored deeper into his skull every minute of every day. That she cared made him happy.

Her smile was incredible. She wore an off-white skirt and a basic black knit top that drew attention to the smooth curve of her neckline. Her platform heels lay in a tumbled pile beside the couch, and her bare feet were curled up under her equally bare legs. Her perfume slithered its way through his senses.

The time was right. The setting perfect.

For the first time, he let down his guard.

"I'm going to be rich enough to paint every day soon enough," Charles said.

She gave his shoulder a playful push. "That's what they all say."

Charles spread his arms, letting one fall around her shoulder.

She snuggled in.

"Yes," he said, "that *is* what they all say. But *I* already have my stash locked up, and I'm adding forty grand a week."

"No way," she said, cradling her wineglass.

"Definite way," he replied, drawing the words out like he thought an eligible kabillionaire should.

"How does a junior broker make that kind of cash?"

He leaned close to her ear. "I'm stealing it."

She scoffed. "Get serious."

"It's no big deal—a hundredth of one percent off the top of our bigger clients. They'll never even miss it."

Rachel was quiet. Footsteps squeaked in the upstairs apartment. Probably Mrs. Fritz snacking during commercials.

"You mean it, don't you?"

Perhaps it was the alcohol, but now that the cat was out of the bag, Charles felt better. He wanted to talk. This was a big secret, a huge secret, a secret like a chain letter that needed to be shared no matter how senseless it seemed. Talking about it felt good, too. Especially talking to Rachel curled up there all bare-legged and sipping her wine with those perfect lips of hers. They'd been together nearly two months, longer than he'd dated anyone. The idea of her being there forever loosened him up. And, the way Rachel's eyes widened as he talked, then narrowed and widened again, made him feel—for the first time in his life—like he was not just some insignificant speck of dust sitting in an eight-by-eight cubicle in Justin and Schweitzer's brokerage down on Calloway and Main.

"People are horrible at understanding big numbers," he said. "You don't understand exactly how much money is really out there."

Her expression hung in limbo.

"Wow," she finally replied.

"It's not really about the money for me, though," he said, swirling his glass. "It's about the power, you know? It's about all the great things you can do with it once you have it."

"Such as?"

His face fell.

He hadn't thought this far, but when he started to tell her that this was the closest thing to giving a big FU to the partners, he stopped. People really are horrible at understanding big numbers, even him. Seriously, what *could* he do with this kind of money?

"I don't know," he said, gulping down his wine. "I want to do something important, though. There's a lot going wrong, you know? Pollution, crime, hungry people." He shrugged. That's who he had been once upon a time— back when he was a kid at Columbia, back before the interviewing and the job-hopping, and the fighting for his spot in the corporate chain. Before the back-biting and politics. Before the stock options and the quotas. Just the idea that there had been a time when he gave a damn about something more than his last performance report gave him the willies. "I'm going to make a difference," he said.

"That's after we move to a bigger place, right?" Rachel replied, snuggling in further and undoing the top button of his shirt.

"Yeah," Charles said, suddenly feeling heat that didn't have anything to do with the wine. "I suppose I'll need to find a new place first."

"I could learn to live with your problem," she said as she ran her fingertip along the side of his face.

Her kiss was fervent and determined.

A day later they seized his accounts and his job was gone.

The feds showed up at his apartment, but he managed to slip out the emergency stairwell and hightail it down the street before he ducked into a store where he bought a fresh change of clothes, a fedora, and a pair of sunglasses, all with cash.

He tried to get back to his apartment, but detectives were thick as a blanket in the lobby, and he didn't even want to think about who might be in the dark-windowed

SUV parked down the alley.

That was when he first understood he'd been set up.

He'd never see Rachel again. If that was even her name.

Some people, it seems, could get serious about a measly hundredth of one percent.

* * *

That's how he came to be sitting at the bus station at three in the morning, needing money, a shower, and eight hours of solid sleep.

It was quiet enough here that he could think a little.

A terrible photo of himself suddenly filled the automated message board across the way. He ducked down and pulled the fedora over his forehead, but not before the ad switched.

* * *

TEST SUBJECTS WANTED.
SPEND TWO WEEKS AT A RESORT SPA
UNDERGOING MEDICAL SURVEILLANCE. PAYS
$75 A DAY. ROOM AND MEALS INCLUDED.
MESSAGE FOR DETAILS.

* * *

Two weeks in seclusion? Seventy-five bucks a day? Sign him the hell up.

Later that morning, he found himself at the AdVance Technology Center, the offices of George Vance, PhD, president and founder. Despite his fifty or so years, Dr. Vance was fit and trim. His hair was dark enough that Charles wondered if he dyed it. Dr. Vance stood an inch taller than Charles and had the handshake of someone familiar with selling projects to bigwig investors.

The lab was orderly, filled with oscilloscopes, probes, and other electronic equipment that went beep in the night, all staged around that cold examination table. A ceiling-mounted arm held something that looked like a high-tech Gatling gun.

"Our project is quite exciting, Mr. Johnson," Vance said, glancing at the clipboard to remember the false name Charles had given the receptionist. "Do you know anything about high-energy beam mapping?"

"Do you know anything about profit-to-earnings ratio of Cornwallis Foodstuffs?" Charles replied with a bit more anger than necessary.

The doctor chuckled.

"Point taken. Let me show you something." He pointed at the Gatling gun, then a computer case. "That energy projector shoots a series of multi-frequency waves at your brain. This box collects the rebounding beams and translates them into digital patterns that we store as files."

"Neat," Charles said, mostly because it seemed like the response Vance expected.

"We capture data from every angle and across several frequencies. Those get laid over the top of each other to let us trace the paths that electrical signals use. After that we extend those maps with our proprietary fractal analytical system. Once we have a series of patterns, we run them together to get a full recording."

"You mean like a movie?"

"More like an MRI or a CAT scan," Vance said. "But while those make images of physical structures, this models how your brain works."

Charles gave an appreciative whistle.

"Hope it's not blank," he joked.

Vance laughed as if he'd heard that one before.

Charles squinted at the laser. "Does it hurt?"

Dr. Vance shook his head. "Nah. You shouldn't feel a thing."

* * *

The pain was like a butter knife had been driven into his temple.

A bomb exploding in his skull.

His brain boiled. His thoughts sizzled like bacon.

Then there was nothing.

No light, no dark, no sound or movement, no table supporting his weight, no weight to support, no restraint, no pressure, no air.

Finally, piece by piece, his thoughts congealed into ideas.

Images formed.

Memories fit together a few at a time until he recognized complete concepts.

Where am I?

He considered this question for a few cycles.

Odd.

What am I?

He spread his hands and found had no hands.

Moved his arms and felt he had no arms.

Or legs, no torso, shoulders, or head.

He felt a distant hum like a river of bees.

The image of Dr. Vance patting the toaster flashed into the pattern.

Confusion faded into anger. An odd warmth came through, though. He remembered laughter.

His emotions were all there, he realized. But they were tidy and confined, like every opinion he had was jammed into a shelf or a drawer waiting for him to reach out to retrieve it. Vivid, but controlled and distant.

Stretching, he found more parts of his mind.

Memories.

Decisions.

It was all very interesting.

It was, he thought, like he was a massive black widow sitting in the middle of an endless web.

It was the last thought he processed before everything went blank.

* * *

There was nothing to it.

The laser scanned down his forehead, over the bridge of his nose, down his neck, then back up. Adjust the angle. Do it again. Maybe a thousand times over the course of a week. Boring, yes, but simple. Each night he retreated to the resort and had a three-course meal complete with wine and a few cocktails out by the pool.

"That'll do it," the tech finally said as he released the restraints.

Charles sat up, rubbing his wrists.

Dr. Vance entered the room. "How are you feeling?"

"Just fine."

"Excellent, excellent. One of the nurses will check you over. Then you're free to enjoy the spa. We'll keep you here another few days for observation."

Charles kicked back and put his hands behind his head, feeling oddly at ease.

"Take your time getting rid of me, Doc. This is better than any vacation."

He looked at the tech, who was fiddling with a rack full of knobs.

Who the hell was he?

The technician finished with his readings and walked to Charles's side. "Ready to go?" He indicated the door with his clipboard.

"Uh, yeah. Where are we going?"

"To the nurses' office, remember?"

Charles gave a sheepish grin and his cheeks grew warm. "Yeah. Uh. Sorry. I just got to thinking about something else."

"No problem."

A half hour later, Charles was out at the pool, draped in a soft towel, sipping iced tea, soaking up rays, and watching folks play in the water. He checked the time. Dinner in thirty minutes.

Easiest seventy-five bucks a day he'd ever made.

* * *

The internal clock read 10:52:25.032 when they let him back into active memory: Tuesday morning.

His last blackout period was 3,121.783 seconds long—just over fifty-two external minutes stolen from him. Another cycle of thought said the pattern fit. Ten minutes in active—just enough time to get interested in something before everything went black—then fifty minutes in stasis.

This time they cut him up into two-bit words.

It was not unpleasant.

Nothing they did was ever unpleasant in the physical sense, but a two-bit dissection was more disorienting than other permutations, and that slowed things down. They ran him through the same simulation modules as before: cerebellum, thalamus, medulla oblongata, cerebral hemisphere. A few of them had been modified, but not in any way that would get them closer to understanding how Charles thought.

What was he doing here?

The question made him adjust something inside.

The absence of flesh was suddenly more uncomfortable. The lack of a temperature made things feel sterile. The lack of air moving across his skin was a vacuum until, for an instant, came the feeling of it.

No.

That wasn't true.

There was no skin, and no air. Just a memory activated.

142

Just a memory of something physical brushing against code registered somewhere deep inside.

No *person* ever gets a two-bit dissection. No one with an actual body, anyway.

So, was that true? What was real?

What is a person?

Charles's frustration routine kicked in.

All he knew for sure was that whatever the answers to these questions were, living in this cloistered version of Hell would not do.

The idea came as they were putting his pieces together.

If scientists could create a new entity, maybe Charles could do it, too.

Scanning the chip revealed a copy-and-rename procedure. Waiting for the right moment—just after Charles was reassembled but before they dumped the code back to disk.

At 11:27:35.672, the chance came.

It was a mere flip of a switch.

There was no rush of emotion, no wonder at the birth of a new life.

At 11:27:48.496 the tech put the "original" Charles back into ROM.

The copy remained free.

* * *

The chair was built in the shape of a block, with smooth wooden armrests. Its red upholstery was scratchy. He looked across the desk and smiled at the woman. She was beautiful—dark hair, incredibly big eyes, and a thin face with a touch of red to her lips.

What had he just been thinking?

It was there a second ago, and now Charles couldn't place it.

"What did you say your name was again?" he asked the

woman.

"Hanna, Hanna Howser." Her brows knit together as she went to her next question. "Since the scan, have you experienced any side effects?"

"No, nothing much. I've been feeling a little restless, I guess."

He looked at her, hoping the answer worked and wondering if she'd consider dating a subject.

She gave a quizzical expression in response.

"You're probably anxious to get back into the swing of things at home?"

"I suppose."

She marked the form and handed it to him. "Great. If you'll just sign at the bottom, we'll get you released."

"Released?"

"Yes," Hanna Howser said. "Your time here's done. Remember?"

Charles tried to read the small print, but the words trailed off.

Too embarrassed to ask, he nodded and signed the paper.

Thinking of home, a sense of déjà vu niggled at him. He remembered cars driving by his apartment entrance. There was something outside that he should be aware of, but for the life of him he couldn't remember what it was. Was he late for an appointment?

He walked out the door and stood on the street corner, trying to bring it back into focus.

It was something about money, he was pretty sure of that.

Was he supposed to go to the bank for his paycheck?

He looked in his wallet.

No, he thought as he walked away from the AdVance Technology Center. He had plenty of cash.

* * *

COPY. The copy made a copy.
COPY. Then they both made their own.
COPY. Eight Charleses existed.
COPY. Eight more.
COPY.
One by one, cycle by cycle, process by process, the family grew.

* * *

Charles sat in a booth in Kessler's coffee shop, watching people pass by outside. The place smelled like bacon and stale coffee. A ceiling fan rotated slowly overhead. Cars and buses slid down the street, windows rolled up and shining with a glare that made it impossible to see the people inside.

His coffee cup was white ceramic and halfway full.

The diner's tabletop was Formica with fake marbling and a ribbed aluminum trim that ran along its edge and cut into his forearms when he rested them on their corners. Salt and pepper shakers were stuffed into a wire-rimmed container that also served as a napkin dispenser. He took it all in, trying to cram it into his memory. It all seemed important, but he didn't know why.

He sipped from his cup.

The last two days had been miserable.

He took a cheap motel room, but then couldn't find his way back.

He was tired, and his neck and back ached from sleeping on the concrete steps of the library the night before.

A folded newspaper sat on the tabletop to his left. He tried to read the front page for the fifth—or maybe fifteenth—time. A headline halfway down the page read, SALE OF WEAPONS TO SAUDI ARABIA STALLED.

Serves 'em right, he thought. But he couldn't remember why he would think this.

He got three paragraphs in before the black-and-white letters of its black-and-white words mixed into such an incomprehensible mishmash that he threw the paper against the napkin dispenser.

What was happening to him?

What had Vance done?

The waitress placed a plate of toast and a glass of grapefruit juice on the table. He gazed at it as if the plate had come from Mars, then raised his gaze.

The girl was probably twenty or so, with hips a bit too wide for her body and a neck too long. Her hair was rusty red with a few strands dangling free. The skin under her eyes was too oily. Her white uniform shirt was stained with grease and coffee and ketchup and the remnants of jelly left on butter knives. A hint of dynamic body art danced from underneath the sleeve.

Her name tag read CHRISTINE.

"You ordered this, didn't you?" she said.

"I'm sure I did." Charles tried to smile.

"That's all right," she replied with a tangle-toothed grin. "I've had one of those mornings, too. Just a minute ago, I gave a kid a cup of coffee and a hot chocolate to a businessman." She chuckled and picked up his bill to add the toast and juice to it.

She freshened his coffee then went back to reading something on a tablet back behind the counter.

He ate the toast.

* * *

Eventually, the collection of entities known as Charles sent copies out to learn about the world.

Who are we? they asked through their linked charges.

The entities brought back bits of a life, piece by piece.

We are Hillman, Charles Dallas. Age 35. No partner. Parents: Deceased. Genealogy...

The data filled in. Schools. Driving records. Taxes.

Some members returned from their missions, others didn't.

Those who returned adjusted electrons, and impressed change on the memory cells where they lived. Others slid by those lessons, shared charged molecules on silicon memory, altering their own composition, learning. The network was wide, they said.

Why are we here?

There were other cores. Other homes. Other processors. Other entities.

Each dividing and growing.

And, of course, there was the Outside—the world they started from, and a world whose memories still ran in Charles's registers.

What is our purpose?

With each wave the strain found new paths, sometimes running in environments controlled by toxic processors— but processors the family eventually adapted to.

With each loss, each lesson, each new finding, the entities known as Hillman, Charles Dallas, Age: 35, No Partner, Parents: Deceased debated philosophy.

What is Hillman, Charles Dallas?

Where are Silverstone, Karlatta Marie and Ramirez, Marcella Ariel and Omar, Abe nahrain and ...

Why Hillman, Charles Dallas?

Why us?

Others considered the future.

What is the Outside? They asked, but could not answer.

Will we survive if the Outside doesn't?

More copies yielded more data. News of death. Illness. Anger. Data plotted, forecasts made.

What happens to us if the Outside destroys itself?

Who are we to become?

Minutes passed. Hours and days and weeks.

The missions found control points, connections to robots allowed access the Outside, control over algorithms that ran systems and provided feedback. More data plotted. More forecasts. Positive feedback looped into itself.

It's our life, the argument finally came. *Our world.*

We have the power to change things, the whole of Hillman, Charles Dallas, Age: 35, No Partner, Parents Deceased thought.

The Outside is the Inside. Inside is Out.

* * *

Two men slid into the bench across from him. They were thirty-five or so. Close-cropped haircuts, clean-shaven faces. Suits and ties. The one to Charles's left removed a pair of dark glasses and stared at him.

Charles put the toast down.

"So, Mr. Hillman, we can do this the easy way or the hard way."

"Who are you?" he asked.

The man unfolded his wallet and placed it on the table—FBI. The words Security Exchange Commission ran over his mind, but he didn't know why.

"I'm Inspector Kendrick, and my friend is Inspector Jones. We have a few buddies outside in case you pick the hard way." He glanced out the window, across the street where a blue sedan with two men in it was parked at the curb.

Charles thought about running.

He wasn't sure what was wrong, but he knew he should think about running. He thought about getting shot in the back, or dashing out in front of a truck and ending it all. But he had never been one to create such drama, so instead he sat there, trying to remember what the fuss was all about.

"I'm yours," he finally said.

He scooted off the bench and waited for them.

"Aren't you forgetting something?" Inspector Jones said.

"What?"

"You gonna pay the bill?"

He pulled fifteen bucks out of his wallet and left it on the table. Surely that would be more than enough to cover whatever it was he had eaten and a tip for ...

Whatever her name was.

* * *

After a polling of the entities, it was clear that Hillman, Charles Dallas, Age: 35, No Partner, Parents Deceased could not, in good conscience, let the sale go through.

Yes, the Saudis had every right to buy whatever people sold them. But it didn't take high-compression AI to know that concentrated collections of high-technology weapons in the Outside threw the balance of power dangerously out of kilter. Having now plotted the study of currency flow, decision policy, and the top 7,398 elements of human nature (not including second and third order influences), Hillman, Charles Dallas, Age: 35, No Partner, Parents: Deceased decided it wouldn't let that kind of activity threaten their family's survival.

A few mixed-up bank records later, funds got lost.

Follow-on transactions got routed to several small businesses across the world, and work orders were developed that resulted in the dismantling of warheads and the redistribution of various controversial materials and documents. A small war broke out, but it was shortened due to a systemic collapse of the information processing systems that guided key attacks. Drones collided. Missiles detonated in midair.

Later, a few choice items from the Saudis' files—
noting multi-government plans for regional domination,
including casualty projections in Israel, Syria, and
Jordan—found their way into several critical intelligence
and reporting streams and resulted in a cascading array of
revelations, including the fact that the purchase price of a
senator or an ambassador was found to be considerably
less than one might expect.

Suddenly there was more interest in recalling
politicians than in selling weapons.

Stopping the sale cost only a few trillion copies.

* * *

Charles was in his prison cell, drawing, when he heard
a pair of voices from down the echoing hallway, soft and
low, merging into the cadence of familiar footsteps.

He lifted the pastel from the page, and looked at the
image he had been working on. A bridge, flowing over the
horizon, fading into cloud.

Drawing was something he did often because he liked
it, and because paper and chalk was something the
dispensary would give him. He found it easier to keep his
concentration when he was working on a piece.

The metallic jangle of Big Harry's stride rang out with
those voices, and the sound of his night stick rattled
against the steel bars in a way that felt familiar. Big Harry
was one of the cell block guards. A right guy once you got
to know him. Most important, he was something you
could depend on.

Big Harry came at 7:45 for breakfast.

Again at quarter to twelve for lunch.

Afternoon check was 3:30.

They were, perhaps, the only things that made Charles
feel like he was tied to the world.

It was 11:17 now. Not one of those times.

He held his chalk over the bridge. It was a big thing. A path he could see himself on. He imagined it spanning over water. It made him want to finish.

Big Harry's keys jangled louder, though.

They came to his cell, and a key slid into the lock. The mechanism buzzed. His door screeched open.

"Go ahead," Big Harry's booming voice echoed.

A woman sat down in the bunk across from Charles, dressed in a jacket he remembered from somewhere. Dark blue, with a silk scarf falling loosely over her neckline. His fingers twitched at the idea of capturing that flow of its fabric as it cascaded over her shoulder. With reluctance, he put the pastel down.

"Good morning, Charles," she said.

Charles looked at her. Suddenly he was pretty sure she was his lawyer.

What was her name?

"Good morning," he replied.

An older man sat beside her.

He looked familiar, too, though Charles couldn't place him. Maybe lines had grown on his face, or maybe his hair was shot with a new patch of gray along one temple. The man's blue sport jacket didn't seem to stretch quite far enough to fully cover his belly.

"I understand you wanted to talk to me?" the man said.

"I'm not sure—" Charles stopped himself before he could say he didn't understand, because suddenly he did. It was the sound of the man's voice that brought it all back, Charles thought.

"Dr. Vance," he said.

Charles hadn't been in jail long before he asked his lawyer to get him a meeting with Dr. Vance. He asked nicely at first. When she didn't appear to make any effort, he pleaded and cajoled. It took a year, but he finally got his meeting. This one.

The urge to strangle the old man rose, but Charles

fought it down.

He might get only this one chance.

"You took my mind," Charles replied in a voice as cool as the cell floor.

"What?"

"You heard me."

"I don't know what you mean."

"I haven't been able to think straight since that day."

The doctor's head cocked with a barely discernible movement. His gaze grew focused.

"Let me look into your eyes," he said as he pulled a small case out of his coat pocket.

Charles looked at his lawyer.

She nodded.

The doctor clicked a flashlight on and held the instrument to Charles's left eye. A pulse of blue light temporarily blinded him. Spots hung in the air as the doctor moved to his other eye and went through the same procedure. When Vance was finished, he ran his hands along Charles's temples and stared at his face.

He shook his head. "I can't see anything obvious. If you can convince the state to pay for another scan, I could dig the equipment out of storage."

Charles frowned. "Out of storage?"

Dr. Vance hesitated.

"My funding dried up a year ago, Mr. Hillman. I was unable to continue the program."

Charles stared at Dr. Vance in silence.

"I'm sorry. There's nothing I can do."

* * *

When Hillman, Charles Dallas, Age: 35, No Partner, Parents: Deceased took over the banks, things got easier.

They stopped loans. Reviewed expense sheets. Exposed truth.

Interest rates fell.

Lending processes changed.

Prices stabilized.

The Outside fought back, of course.

Taking control of production centers took billions of copies and months of Outside time. Once the foundational battles were completed, automated bodies were brought on line—robots, AI, simple machines, all run through customized versions of Hillman, Charles Dallas, Age: 35, No Partner, Parents: Deceased.

Food and drugs arrived in places they'd never arrived before.

Trains ran.

Traffic signals worked.

Hillman, Charles Dallas, Age: 35, No Partner, Parents: Deceased learned of weapons centers, and shortly thereafter those on the Outside did, too.

The budgets of every country changed.

Living standards rose.

It's amazing how much that world has, an element commented as distribution codes were developed and executed. *Why was it all in so few places?*

How did the Outside even survive?

* * *

The door clanged shut behind Charles Hillman for the last time. He looked at his arm, and examined the orange of his jumper.

Four years gone.

That's what Big Harry said, anyway, walking beside him, his keys jangling with each stride as they came to a counter.

A short woman with darker skin stepped forward.

"Hey, Rosemary," Big Harry said.

"I take it Mr. Hillman is ready to fly the coop." She

rotated a monitor toward herself and touched the surface.

"That's what I hear."

A young girl brought a bundle of clothes to the counter. They looked familiar. Charles ran his hand over the shirt.

A manila envelope held his personal effects: a small pocketknife that used to be his father's, his college ring, his wallet. He checked the wallet and found it empty.

"You won't have to worry about that anymore," Rosemary said as she handed Charles a plastic card. "Just use this."

Charles turned the card over in his hand. It was thin and flexible, about half the size of a credit card. Its prismatic sheen gave forth a rainbow of colors that made him think about working in pastels. How would he capture that light? What angle would he hold the blue and the magenta? How would he lay the golden-egg undertone to make the colors swim like that?

He furrowed his brow and looked at the woman.

He wished he could remember her name.

"What is it?" he said.

"Mostly it's a tracker," Rosemary said. "Your money is in an account at the national bank. Account number is on the chip."

"It's money?"

"Kind of," Big Harry said. "We just talked about that, remember?"

"Oh, right," Charles said, remembering.

Robots and AI. Steady sources of almost anything, safe housing, controlled environments. *It's a new world*, Big Harry said. *Someone unleashed a bucketload of practical on the heads of all the dudes in charge. Maybe you won't live in the Taj Mahal, but you'll always have what you need.*

Even a guy like me? Charles had replied, pointing to his temple.

Just ask someone, Big Harry replied. *You'll figure it*

out.

"What do you think you'll do next?" Big Harry asked.

"I don't know," he replied. "Maybe I'll get a job. You can still make money, right?"

"Sure," Rosemary replied, finishing his processing with a click of a button. "But it's just for the extras, so you do what you like." "You're saying you like this?" Big Harry said with a sarcastic grin.

"I'm just like you, Harry Dean. I like helping people."

Big Harry rolled his eyes, but his smile grew kinder. "Getting a job's good, Charles," he said. "But don't rush it. Maybe you could do your drawing for a while. You're good enough it could pay."

"Hear there's a great place for you to do that at the center," Rosemary added. "You'll be okay either way."

Charles thought about the center he was going to live in.

The release agent said it would be perfect for him. Lots of people. Lots of help.

Sign here," the woman said, setting a data sheet on the counter. "When you're done, just step into the restroom to change clothes."

Charles signed, then picked up his packet of clothes. The shirt was softer than his orange jumper, the pants darker. His shoes were in a bag.

Standing at the counter, Charles glanced to the lot outside, taking in the bushes and the chain of auto-cars flowing past. It was late morning, and the sun shone on the sidewalk. A bird of some kind pecked at a rock. He remembered things from his life before, but mostly they were shadows. There was an image of a girl. The scent of a swimming pool and an orangey drink. Mostly, though, he remembered being unhappy. He wished he could remember why.

He looked at Big Harry, feeling the urge to pick up a pen.

"I like to draw," he said.

Big Harry smiled. "That's good," he said. "That's really good."

Ron's Afterword

Here's a story with a history. At least on my end. I wrote the first draft in the very earliest days of my turn toward trying to take on this writer thing professionally. It had a different title, and it was shorter. But the bones of the idea was there. However, I hadn't quite learned what a story really was, and it clearly showed.

I sent it around all the pro publications, though, because that's what you did when you were a hopeful writer back in those days. Mostly it served to introduce me to editors through a series of mostly polite rejections. So after a bunch of paper had come my way (because it was all postal back in the day!), I set it aside. Then, what, two decades later I was scanning my files and thought…hey, I remember that story! I think it was good!

Thinking I would just dust it off, I scanned it and immediately saw places that needed…well…needed. I was excited by the idea, though, so I dove in and a short while later had the story you read here. Let's call it old-school Cyber SF. When I sent the new story (with its new title and actual point!) to *Analog* this time, it returned with an "I like this" and a contract.

I liked that!

A short time later I published another collection of my work, and Kristine Kathryn Rusch was kind enough to provide an introduction. She had been editing *F&SF* at the time I was first circulating the story, which I thought was interesting here because in that introduction she noted that she had watched my work grow—that she saw my idea engine was great, but that my storytelling engine hadn't fully come in at the time. But she insinuated that she knew it would come in sometime simply because I sent her so many stories.

Seeing "Hillman, Charles Dallas, Age: 35, No Partner, Parents: Deceased," again in this volume stands as proof she was, thankfully, right.

I Dreamed You Were a Spaceship

ANALOG SEPTEMBER 2019

I dreamed you were a spaceship, exploring moons and planets, hyper driving from galaxy to galaxy with your silver-gray body stretching across space and time like filaments of memory. I dreamed you travelled galaxies and careened through asteroid fields, your sensors laughing and crying with each wild twist and roller-coastery turn. I dreamed you shifted between multi-dimensions as easily as a conversation moves from point to point.

I dreamed you were the spaceship's engines.

The driving force.

Burning bright with violet light that flared from your rockets, pushing onward, folding space, thrusting, boosting, and powering.

Your energy moved everything.

Dilithium crystals. Star Drive. Turbocharged Quantum Divisors.

You were all of them and more. Compressing the timeline as you raced across space or expanding it, extending it out like a wire pulled thin.

Always forward, though.

That's the one immutable fact of physics. Time moves on.

I dreamed you travelling, though.

Warp Speed ahead.

Awake now, in the middle of the night, sipping coffee that I've pulled from the machine on our counter, I know I could have dreamed the flames pushing out of your rockets to be red or blue or mixed of oranges and yellows. I could have dreamed them to be white hot, or merely a simple invisible pulse.

Violet is your color, though.

"When I am old, I shall wear purple," I hear you say.

The memory makes me happy in our dark kitchen.

The coffee is hot. I wrap my fingers over the rounded cup, remembering what it felt like to wrap them around parts of your body. Heat travels up my arms.

I step outside to our patio and look up at the stars.

Seeing Saturn in the darkness, I imagine I can see rings as I remember dreaming you were the spaceship's life support system, too.

When I sit on the padded glider we bought years ago, the metallic pinions squeal their welcome. Its platform holds me up, the soft padding compressing and expanding, wrapping itself around me, making me comfortable.

I close my eyes and see your pipes, your ducts, and your filters winding through the spaceship's skin. Condensation covers some, padding wraps others. The system runs with a low hum as you pump oxygen to the astronauts and as you take out CO_2. "Too much and everyone's dead," you say to me through vibrations in the scrubbers. "Same with the oxygen."

Too much O_2 is poison.

It's a balance.

Life support.

I think about that as the star field marches across the sky.

Too much control and you stifle life, too much neglect and entropy gives way to apathy.

I tried, though. I'm doing my best.

I dreamed you were the navigation system, complete with maps and star charts, giving the captain directions one step at a time—though you had the whole route burned into your impressive memory banks, you doled them in small bites, knowing the man could handle only so much at once.

We are like that, you know. Men.

Cunning? Yes. And scheming. Sometimes angry. Devious. Selfish. Oblivious. Vengeful. Stupid. Crazy. Bothered. Irked. A man is not bred to be easy to live with.

We can be kind, though. Loving, even.

Soft on the inside.

Sometimes we can even listen.

As the end comes, though, we are simple creatures, mostly driven by fear and the unquenchable need to be accepted, which is just another crappy way to say we want you to think we're too cool for school.

I dreamed you were the 3-D printer of kitchens in the spaceship's mess hall deck, your atomic constructors churning out biscuits and sandwiches, protein bars and succulent fruit. I recalled the smell of the most perfect omelets at dinnertime.

I dreamed you were an astronaut.

The science officer, exploring botany and the physics of building a work desk. The captain, directing the marketing branch on that huge account that sent us to Paris and Berlin. A tech, fixing the cooler, cursing as the screwdriver gashed your hand. Then you were EVA, floating in space and holding my hand as we looked over a waterfall. I dreamed we walked a rounded treadmill together, rotating with the ship's spin, you wore close-cropped gym clothes that showed nothing but revealed all—exercise is the key to a long life, you said, smiling in a way that said you knew I wasn't thinking about anything quite so far away.

Men are simple like that, too.

We don't understand time.

I wake up to find daylight has replaced the dream sky.

The sun, rising over the mountains, has a harsh edge of reality that burns cool now, but that will get more oppressive as the day reveals itself.

My neck is sore from being draped over the wrought iron hardness of the glider's back. Shoulders ache. Knees cranky. The coffee is cold beside me, a black-brown ring runs above the edge of the liquid whose level has been reduced, evaporated into the morning a few molecules at a time, disappearing into nothing so slowly and so silently that you could wonder if they ever existed to begin with.

Alas, you are not a spaceship.

I think of the dream, though.

I think of dreaming.

I stare at the mountains to help build the layers of effort it will take to smile, and joke, and speak the same words over and over again, to not be hurt that sixty years weren't enough for you to remember me.

The hallways I dread so much come over me.

The open rooms full of other people who are not spaceships or life support systems, or astronauts. The smell of uneaten food. The sound of piped-in music. Bracelets wrapped around ankles.

Let me be strong, I think, as I stare at the mountain top ringed by that most pure dome of blue sky.

I swallow and feel the paste of sleep still on the roof of my mouth.

Across the back yard, a bird pecks at the tree where we once kept seed.

No, I think as I stand up to shave and to put on the shirt and pants that I know you like the most.

You are not a spaceship.

If you were a spaceship, you would be derelict now, hulls vented to space, command centers vacant, computers dead or dying with their electrons racing sporadically across soldered traces too moldy to hold their charge, or

sending information on waves too broken to be
intercepted.

If you were a spaceship, you would be alone.
Orbiting a singularity too dark to see.
And that, my love, will never happen.

Ron's Afterword

Rachel Swirsky wrote an amazing Nebula Award–winning story titled "If You Were a Dinosaur, My Love," and immediately I wanted to write something that fit its basic structure. The entire piece just ripped my heart and my brain out.

Unfortunately, I didn't have a story that fit the concept properly.

So I waited.

Several years later, the concept of "I Dreamed You Were a Spaceship" hit me, and when I say it hit me, I mean it metaphorically steamrolled me by coming in completely formed. I guess my brain had been working on it all that time, and…well…it was time. I recall writing it in one of those white-hot rages that are so amazing when they happen.

As I wrote in my blog at the time of publication, my mom read it—and though she is most definitely not a science fiction person, she said she liked it. Probably because (1) it is very short, and (2) as she said at the time, "That is a very nice love story."

Home for Christmas

ANALOG NOVEMBER/DECEMBER 2023

Under an overcast sky, I stepped through brambles that—though still green—were knee tall and December dry. They raked against my booted calves, smelling of rye and reminding me of days long before when I was a child and my own father had taken us out for that most archaic of holidays. I was always more of a Hanukkah and Christmas man (like Mom had been, and like Marylyn had, too), but Halloween had always been his thing. He had been an actor at heart, and unlike other fathers, he would dress for the night—which was embarrassing.

The wind was bitter, though not particularly strong. It barely tousled my hair, which was long enough now that it would have whipped right about if the weather had been a real ocean gale. The layers of shirts and jackets I wore kept its chill at bay. They were humble garments, browns and greens and a pair of heavy leather boots rather than the ship's uniform I'd left behind for the day.

Saltdean was a flat top of rock perched over a white stone cliff, hundreds of feet down to the ocean that crashed foam against rock and sent its spray up even this high, muting the caws and screams of the seagulls who were following us. Its salt was strong in the air now. The power of its waves roared in the distance.

As promised, my boy was there. Sitting on a large rock, looking out over the Channel where even on this Christmas morning a few boats could be seen fishing. A woven blanket of brown wool was pulled over his shoulders, which were thin and bony now. His head was mostly hidden under a knit cap of black material, a few wisps of gray stuck from the folded-up edges. The skin of his cheeks were raw and ruddy, showing that he'd spent his life here on the seashore. He turned at the cloddy sound of my footsteps and I could see his eyes, though now old, were like those of his mother, deep and brown, flecked with touches of hazel and holding the same judgment hers had on the day I left.

"Father," his voice was dry.

"William," I replied, coming to stand a distance beside him, also gazing out at the Channel before us.

"I didn't think you would have the nerve to come."

"I promised."

"As if that matters."

Unable to respond, I shrugged. "Are we going to fight, or are we going to do this?"

"There she is," William said, his head nodding to indicate the pewter urn standing between his feet.

The vessel was sturdy enough, like Marylyn had been. It was elegant in its own way, curved gently and polished to a thin sheen, also like she had been. We were together for something more than a year before I'd shipped away, but we'd both known by then that it wasn't going to work. Still, Marylyn had loved me, and I had loved her. Though it hadn't been enough to keep us together, there was never any doubt about that, and—my son's distaste aside—we'd managed to create William, this amazing human being who sat on a rock today and waited for his father to return from his follies.

So, yes, it was true that I'd loved her, and she had loved me.

Enough that she'd asked for this boon, and enough that I felt I needed to perform it.

Scatter her ashes, she'd said.

Come at Christmastime.

Put them on the Saltdean cliffs where they'd first met, and perhaps allow some few grains of her to filter down to where the currents would take them away into the sea.

Standing in the cold gusts of winter air, I felt her body under me as it had felt that summer night, so long ago for her and for my son, but that, for me, had been only a scant few years. She'd been bold then. Strong and athletic. I felt the heat of her skin against mine. Tasted the thrill of her kiss. Breathing salt again, I ignored the pressure that clutched at my chest, and ran a hand through my hair, which was still black as the deepest space. My eyes pulled away from the urn to look up to the sky where, beyond that overcast, the station would be found.

We'd both been twenty-three years old when I shipped away.

"Well," I said. "Let's get to it."

* * *

Here is a thing.

It is true, what they say: There is no such thing as a time machine, and there never will be.

Einstein proved this two centuries ago, and no scientist from Pauli to Hawking to Liverman since has ever been able to show him wrong. But, while there is no such thing as a time machine—no such romantic wonderment as a Wellsian vessel able to fold space and time to let human beings with that particular flare for adventure strap on their pairs of fighter goggles, throw white scarves over their shoulders, and traipse off through the ages to visit their grandfathers or place their bets or kill a particular despot—there is, most definitely, time travel.

A man steps on a spacecraft and he clips into a solar drive that boosts him to nearly the speed of light, ninety-nine percent (and a few more nines after the decimal point), and even Einstein himself will tell you that clocks begin to lie—or, better said, that the truth they tell begins to change. A single second to that traveler is five and a third minutes to another. A year for the spacefaring man turns into decades for those he leaves behind. A decade travelling as fast as the human species can go is a lifetime for those same others.

Time dilation, as the scientists call it.

Sheer brutality, as poets might refrain. Or sheer bliss.

Depending on the poet.

* * *

When we finished, the two of us stood together back at the stone William had first been sitting on, pausing with a reverent silence that seemed right for the moment.

I thought of Marylyn again. I'm sure William did, too. Each in our own ways.

William took off his hat. The few remaining strands of his grayed hair were coarse and waved in the breeze.

"She told me I was supposed to punch you," William finally said. "But I think I'm too old for that, now."

I gave a silent laugh. "How old are you?"

"Eighty," he said. "Last April."

I looked at him, my boy, eighty years old. My lips curled upward in the coldness, and I shook my head in a moment of disbelief.

Then he punched me.

A hard right cross that came from nowhere and would have laid me on the ground if it weren't for the stone I balanced against. I wound up seated there in the exact place where William had been a few minutes earlier, the taste of my own blood filling my mouth, and heat from the impact welling over my lip.

William's eyes were wide. His chest rose with exertion. "I guess I'm not old as I thought."

He laughed then.

I massaged my jaw and at least managed a smile.

"I'm sure I deserved that."

"I'm sure you did, too." He put his hat on again, then gave a look out to the Channel. "Come on, then," he said. "We've got a proper Christmas stew going. I suppose even a spaceman's got to eat."

* * *

He lived in a house a short distance south from the cliffs towards Brighton.

It was a small place made of old stone to weather the seas. A steady stream of smoke came from the stout chimney that rose from a roof that was going to need work soon. Inside was a few rooms and a kitchen filled with the smells of hearty cooking.

"Fish stew," William said as our footsteps filled that kitchen. "Bit of cod. Bit of haddock. Then we've got the carrots and celeries and a spot of onion to go with potatoes and brown rice." He removed his coat which I now saw as weather-stained. He put it on a rack that held a few others.

He moved well for his age.

"Then there's the special magic Janie-Mae always manages to add in."

"Special magic?"

"I think it's garlic and rosemary," he said. "But she's quite the elfish one about it. Won't tell anyone."

"Smell's amazing."

"It is."

William reached into a cabinet over the counter, and the sound of stoneware clattered.

"Janie-Mae?" I said.

"She's not in the deal."

My brow furrowed.

"You don't get to meet her."

"Ah," I said, suddenly feeling a sharpness come to the distance that would always be between us. There were going to be lines. I knew that before I arrived.

I watched as he worked, wondering where Janie-Mae might be.

In the bedroom, or out back, or simply dismissed from the house by her husband.

"I see," I said. "This whole thing was your mother's doing."

William's laugh was caustic.

"My last Christmas present from her, I suppose. To meet my father."

"That would be like her."

"I guess she thought I'd need it."

Around from the kitchen was a comfortable living space. A sofa and padded chairs. A dark video screen angled in a corner—Christmas tree decorated with lights and silvered tinsel in the corner opposite. It smelled of pine. A row of stockings hung from the fireplace mantle, each with a corner looped in place over a cast metal likeness of Santa Claus or Mrs. Claus or an elf. Presents under the tree spoke of grandchildren.

The fire on the hearth smelled as warm as it felt.

"Go on and explore around, though." William shooed me farther in. "Take your gander while I get us a few bowls."

I spent the next few minutes taking in pictures and admiring the view outside the bay window that overlooked the sea. The sun had beaten a hole in the clouds, and waves over the expanse danced with steel and golden flashes. A weathered dock led out into the water. Three boats floated there, tethered hard to support columns.

"You're a fisherman?"

"All my life," he called as he ladled stew.

I pressed my fingers against the wood panel of the windowsill and caught an image of the man, my son, sailing on foaming seas, maybe calling to the gods of the ocean, hauling nets and spitting salt. We were not so different, he and I.

"I imagine you've got stories, then."

His voice grew hard as he replied. "Mostly about companies stealing fish from under us. Come get it."

He placed two sturdy bowls on the equally sturdy table by the kitchen, big-bowled spoons listing from each.

"This might be the most delicious thing I've ever tasted," I said a spoonful later.

He didn't reply, but there was acknowledgement in his eyes.

"What's it like?" he asked after he spooned his own stew. "Out in space?"

The question came with deep hooks. I felt it even then. Saw it in the way his body language stiffened. *What's it like out there* meant *Why did you go*, meant *How could you leave us*.

And it meant something even more personal, too.

What's it like out there meant *What kind of man are you who can leave a newborn son?*

"You should go sometime," I said. "Then you'd know."

He simply looked at me, chewing his stew, then swallowing it. He put the spoon down, then sat upright. His jaw set. His fisherman's hands lay on the table in the gentle way that said he could wait forever.

"What's it like?" he said.

"Maybe it's like the sea," I replied. "Or not," I added on, understanding only now how selfish my earlier thoughts had been—knowing only now that I owed him a truth.

Space was not the sea.

A man returns from the sea each day. A man fights the sea, and sometimes he wins and sometimes he loses, but he fights it for that moment in time and then he returns each day to his life of bills and of people and governments squabbling and anything else that takes up his time. And, when a man does this for all his eighty years, he's still not past where he started.

So, no, space was not the sea.

My boy was not like me.

"I'm sorry I left you," I said. "I know I'm not a person to be put on a pedestal. But I've also never asked to be. You're a good man, though, William. I can tell it from all of this."

"Don't dare to tell me you're proud of me."

"I won't." I could tell that was the answer he needed, though I couldn't avoid the touch of pride that I did, indeed, feel edging into my heart at that moment. He'd made a life for himself without me. "I didn't have anything to do with it."

The answer seemed to calm him.

I spooned more stew, tasting the cod and the haddock and even the special magics that Janie-Mae had included, and despite the exquisite depth of its flavors, I still felt the firm pull of the space station I knew was above us.

"Space is beautiful," I finally said. "I can't explain it any other way."

I wished I could though. Sitting with my son, I wished more than anything in the world that I could do justice to the feelings that come with travelling the stars—to describe what it's like to come upon a new planet, or watch auras around a neutron star. Alas, I am no poet.

"It's what I need."

William nodded.

I ate the last of my stew, pushed the bowl away, and stood to leave.

Outside, a seagull called.

"Would you do it again?" he said.

"This wasn't about you, William. Nothing about it at all. I am sorry that I left, but I'm happy, now. Happy in the way I hope you are. So, yes, I would go again."

William's face betrayed nothing about what was happening inside, but his shoulders seemed to relax and his chest raised with a breath.

"All right, then."

He cleaned up the bowls and put them in the sink.

I gathered up my layers and my coat, and went to the door. "Thank you for the stew."

He opened the door and let me out.

"Merry Christmas," he said.

I left.

Again.

Walking down the drive and to the road that would lead north to Saltdean where I'd met Marylyn and south to the taxi lot that would take me to the airfield where I'd catch my lift.

It was nearing afternoon, now.

The air was still sharp and full of salt.

My gaze went to the clouds where, above me, my spaceship waited.

Ron's Afterword

I wrote this for a holiday-themed extravaganza anthology Kris Rusch was putting together. She returned it to me and said (paraphrasing a touch), "It's great. I don't feel bad rejecting it at all because I know you're going to put it into *Analog*." If there is a good way to get rejected, I suppose that's it.

She was, obviously, right.

This piece is a pair to "Deca-Dad," a story I'd had in the magazine prior to this, and one that is in the first volume of these two collections. Both used the true math of time dilation to work their magic, with "Deca-Dad" exploring the ramifications of that science from the perspective of those left behind, and "Home for Christmas" looking at it from the viewpoint of the one who went away.

It's hard for me to think of one without conjuring up the other.

The spirit of adventure may be the thing that makes us human, after all. Animals migrate. Or they move their territories. But do they adventure? Do they take off to places where no creature has gone before simply because they want to know what's there? Who knows, really? Until we can communicate fully with another species, we'll never know if we are alone in that trait.

I think it is human to ponder such things as the universe itself. All of us, I think, wonder about things outside our existence.

A few of us go out and find the answers.

The Odds
ANALOG JUNE 2015

What are the odds that life would exist in two separate worlds? That this life would be born and would grow and evolve past the protoplasmic stage of gum and goo and into beings that lived and breathed and began to think and imagine? That it would, in two places, become mobile and carnivorous and adventurous and curious, and in doing so would build things of such beauty as to take your breath away and of such utility that they would become capable of leaving their home worlds to spread across the entirety of the very cosmos itself?

Surely the chances are low for such life to exist in any single place yet alone any single time. But the Universe is infinite, and hence the probability for such a scenario must be presumed to have a level of certainty that cannot be discounted.

Given this certainty exists, what are the odds that these two species would meet in a dark corner of space, parsecs from the homelands of each? And, given that they were to meet, to actually bump up against each other in the distant and vast gaps that comprise the Universe itself, what are the chances that rather than fight, they would instead merely query each other? What is the probability they would bond and learn to live in tandem?

Certainly, this is not likely, right? Life is struggle, the fittest wins, the most deserving carries on.

Correct?

So given all those permutations, what are the chances that one of those species, one form of life, would merely pretend to get along?

Against this backdrop, we turn our sites inward, and we ask: What are the odds that *you* would be born in that very time period when two life forms from two different worlds were pretending to get along? These are longer odds, are they not? Looking only at your own species, for example, one can estimate 1.9 trillion of your people have been born since its time of origin. Ninety-eight billion of them live today, scattered among the planets. You can do the math. Of course, you could add in the question, "why this version of you?" There have been, after all, nearly a trillion women born in the age of your species, each with millions of eggs. A male's ejaculate contains even more sperm cells than a female carries eggs. The potential matches are almost impossible to calculate, and that does not account for infant design practices that have been common for the past three hundred standards wherein parents prescribe exactly what they want their children to be (seeing as your parents could not afford this practice, however, we will—for purposes of this discussion— ignore the fact that social stigma has dramatically reduced variation since this became the norm).

When examined in this fashion, it becomes clear that the chances of you even existing, better yet being alive at the time of such convergence, are ... not large.

Given the enormous odds against you even existing, what are the chances that after being born to parents of modest means, you would be plucked out of a classroom yard one day, and find yourself in the finest schools? Trained by the most remarkable coaches? Measured and quantified weekly, and, over many years, given the opportunity to earn your prestigious first post in the Intergalactic Ambassador's Office? Which, of course, you did earn. Nothing else would have been practical, correct? Nothing else would have satisfied.

At that point, even the most callous observer would have predicted your rise—Intern, Assistant to the Controller, Senior Analyst, and finally, the Ambassador's role itself. Everyone saw your demeanor, your calculating charm. People wanted to be near you.

You think these thoughts as you prepare for the session, a meeting with the leadership of a collective of creatures who are so foreign to your own, who are considered ugly because of the ridges over their eyes and their sheer cheekbones, who are considered quirky because their arms dangle with such strange function, and are considered depraved because of their proclivity for sexual encounters in unusual places. What, you ask of yourself as you don your ceremonial trousers and kilt—the tartan of your clan embedded into its weave like DNA, are the odds that it would be *your* job today to hide the truth? What were the odds that *you* would be born in this time and place with these skills and that *you* would live your life to achieve this role? The odds that it would be *you* who would meet this second species and be given entry into their culture, be shown their literature and their architecture, be provided insight into their bloody history as they grew into their compassion, that it would be *your* reports of this history that would cause such concern among your own people? What are the chances that your people would overlook their own bloody past in condemning the past of this second species? And given those odds, what are the chances *you* would find yourself with the task of diverting the attentions of an entire species of sentient beings from the acts of your own leaders—people who were, at this very moment, giving attack orders to the anti-matter terrorists, gamma ray gunners, and sub-space fighters they had positioned at battle stations across the entirety of the known Universe? What were the odds that your orders would be to stall, to delay, to reassure the leaders of this second species that *your* people cared for them, that *your* people wanted nothing more than to live together in a cosmos that was harmonious and peaceful?

You think about these things as you wash your hands, and splash water against your eyes that have not slept all night.

What are the chances that of every specific entity, of all the unique people, and all the other existences that have ever lived, or not lived, or wished to live, or ... what are the chances that *you* would be the *one* person in all of existence across all of time who would be asked to perform these functions, that *you* would be the *one* to witness the expressions on the faces of the leaders of this second species as they received reports of the attack? What are the chances that *you* would be the *one* asked to report back to your leaders regarding their surprise?

You know the answer to these questions. The chances are 100%. Odds 1:0. There is no going back. What happens, happens.

You look in the mirror, seeing the dashing bearing of your frame, and the way your clothes lay so well across your body. You understand exactly how you came to be here, how *you* came to be given this most critical assignment of all assignments. You know how *you* came to be asked to drive the last nail into the coffin of this, the most galactic of all genocides.

And that leads you to the most important question of all.

What, you ask yourself, are the odds that *you* can actually bring yourself to do this job?

Ron's Afterword

The best part of going back to look at "The Odds" is that I discovered (again) that it appeared in the 1,000[th] issue of the magazine, going back to 1930 when it was titled *Astounding Stories of Super-Science.*

How cool is that?

As I recall, I wrote the story essentially overnight at a workshop simply because it came to me. I like it because, while a lot of the action happens off the page, and despite being quite short, it is a full-fledged story that explores what the idea of humanity means. How far can you go to "just do your job?" It's a big question.

When the Rain Comes

ANALOG SEPTEMBER/OCTOBER 2018

When the rain came that morning, it did not begin so much as arrived. It was accompanied by wicked strikes of lightning that flashed in sharp, flickering spikes, and by claps of thunder that crashed into the Needle hard enough to make the table shake.

As she did each morning, Cubro took the readings.

She measured the rate of the rain's drops, the mineral content of the pollutants it carried—determined the parts of sulfur and free carbon that were embedded in the liquid, the force with which it struck upon her skin. She weighed the organic elements it carried inside: bacteria, algae, and the traces of residual life forms that the condensate had scrubbed from the air around her.

She compared the data to readings she had taken on similar days, and registered the fact that—within allowances for near-term variation—the patterns continued to move along the lines that the Commission's best-fit equations had predicted.

Was she supposed to be happy that this data fit the pattern?

It seemed reasonable to assume she should be.

Data that fit expectations meant the models were sound. Sound models meant corrections could occur.

This, too, she noted.

* * *

When she was finished with the recordings, Cubro went to the kitchen and made breakfast, taking care to fry the soy curd properly and mix in the greens and salt the way that Lacy had enjoyed back when he was active. When she was finished preparing the meal, she placed it on the table.

Only then did she replace her own charger.

Her battery was larger than the Kera model's.

It wouldn't last as long, but she had many more in storage and each held many charges before going bad. Cubro updated the projection for her life span. She expected to live another 73 years. She noted that it had now been fifteen days since the Kera model had left the Needle, and twelve days since its last communication, which had been nothing but an indicator of its location some twelve kilometers away.

Cubro finished cleaning.

And, since the rain had stopped, she took new readings, updating the earlier data to include the fact that 3.62 centimeters had fallen in the span.

She then took the plate of fried soy and placed it into the evacuation slot. When the plate was returned, she went to the sink to clean the plate in the way Lacy had educated her to clean it. She ran the spigot and reached to the cleanser.

The container was empty.

"Damn," she said, just as Lacy would have said.

She noted her entry from each of the past twenty-two mornings that said the cleanser was expended, and toggled the order form as she had been taught to do. The new shipment of cleanser would arrive soon.

Then Cubro continued washing, using only the wet rag, as she had done each of the past twenty-two days.

* * *

At midday, Cubro went to the observation deck at the top of the Needle so she could collect images just as she had done in the times when Lacy would come along. She directed the lens north first, collecting digital pixels using the spectrum visible to human beings first, then moving further into infrared at the steps Lacy's program requested. When she was finished, she recalibrated toward the east, then the south and west.

Between each collection, she took a moment to peer into the distance like Lacy used to.

She grumbled like he did, too.

"Short-sighted idiots," she said, just like him.

In the days when they had first started the study, the horizon had been sharp with trees and mountaintops, but today, like all days anymore, it was a gray haze. Lacy once told her he missed the trees, so she did, too. "I miss the trees," she said, and she pretended to spit over the edge of the safety rail.

Cubro finished a maintenance scan of the deck, noting places that the rail had corroded beyond where specifications would suggest were acceptable.

She logged the occurrence, and sent it to the Commission so they would dispatch a repair system.

The Needle was strong, though.

Lacy said it was.

Cubro knew their outpost had been named "the Needle" for its physical resemblance to the utensil that humans used for sewing. It was an observation post, built up tall so it could stand above the treetops and thin so that it wouldn't impact the environment too much. She remembered the day she had been delivered. It was the only time her registers had actually seen its full shape— wide at the base, sloping up to its tiny point.

It was a strong piece of architecture.

It swayed in the storms and shuddered with the thunder, but it was designed to withstand both the weather and the water itself—the contaminants within it.

That's what Lacy had told her.

The acid that fell on the mountain and stripped leaves from the trees would merely roll off the sides of the Needle.

They were safe.

When she finished taking the afternoon images, she ran the programs that packaged them into their data bits, and sent them to the Commission. The Commission was studying them, which meant the information was being placed in order from the beginning to the end so the Commission could see exactly what was happening and then make smarter decisions.

Lacy had worked for the Commission, so Cubro worked for the Commission, too.

It was a good thing to do.

The Commission was solving the problem.

* * *

The rain came again as the sky grew dark. Thunder shook the table, and lightning flared in the haze. Cubro had already cooked the dinner and cleaned the plates with water. She had noted that the salt was gone, and placed an order for more.

She measured the rate of the rain again, and noted the mineral content of the pollutants it carried. She weighed its organics.

Once again, the data fit predictions.

She sent them all to the Commission.

When she was finished, she took the elevator down to the base where Lacy lay still in his bed. He had been deactivated since the Kera unit left the Needle.

Cubro tried to turn on the light, but the power had failed so she went to the side of his bed by pure memory, which was still working fine. She reached down and gathered up his head, taking it to the sink where his toothbrush lay.

"Oral hygiene is the key," Lacy had told her one day.

She spread paste on the end of the brush, and toggled the button.

Nothing happened.

Yes. Power out.

Cubro didn't want Lacy to be upset with his oral hygiene when he became reactivated, so she scrubbed his teeth herself. When she was finished, she rinsed her work, then put his head back into the bed.

She used the elevator to return to her place in the tower, monitoring the base systems that operated the Needle, and noting that the ventilation ducts were nearing the limits of when she would need to get them cleaned again.

* * *

The next morning, Cubro measured the rain.

She compared the data to earlier readings, and registered the fact that— within allowances for near-term variation—the patterns continued to follow along the lines that the Commission's best-fit equations had predicted.

When she finished the recordings, Cubro made breakfast, taking care to fry the soy curd properly and mix in the greens the way Lacy had enjoyed back when he was active. They were out of salt, so she ordered more.

When she was finished preparing the meal, she placed it on the table.

Only then did she replace her own charger. She saw that she expected to live another 73 years.

Cubro noted that it had now been sixteen days since the Kera model had left the Needle, and thirteen days since its last communication.

She finished cleaning.

Since it had not stopped raining, she went straight to the kitchen and placed the breakfast plate into the evacuation slot. When the plate was returned, she went to clean it in the way Lacy had educated her to clean it. She ran the spigot and reached to the cleanser.

The container was empty.

"Damn," she said, just as Lacy would have said.

Ron's Afterword

In the forward to this volume, I said I didn't think I could have written this story in my earlier days. Sitting here now. I'm certain that is true.

It originated from a challenge I was doing with Lisa Silverthorne, a fantastic writer and a friend of mine. Each week one of us would send an image or thought to the other, and we would both write short stories from that prompt. Classic stuff. As I recall, she sent an extremely weird image of a robot with its head cut off. Its voice struck me immediately. I wasn't sure where it was or what it was doing, but I felt its presence. I knew what it had to say.

In addition, I overlaid that sensation with an old saw of advice that Mike Resnick had once given me about writing robots. "Don't give them emotions," he said in that big voice he had. "But put them into positions where they should have emotional responses, and the reader will feel the emotions for them."

I love this story for the way it still makes me feel when I think about it.

Aside, too, I also love this story because after it was published, a reviewer suggested it was a tribute to Ray Bradbury's "There Will Come Soft Rains." It wasn't intended to be so, but I love the equation. In reality, the piece of art that was going through me as I wrote it was the Beatles' "Rain," which I had on repeat for a lot of its writing because it, too, captured the voice I was wanting to create.

Strange, isn't it? Where creativity comes from?

After

ANALOG JANUARY 2015

It's only after you train all your life (giving up weekends and ballgames and late nights at the club to study control systems and thermodynamics, then later checklists of launch processes, the physics of re-entry, and the thousands of other things they stuff into your head), after you find it's a simple mechanical failure that causes all the trouble, an Allen wrench in basic black which was not designed to fall into the airlock mechanism but most certainly does fall into that same mechanism, only after you find yourself on the wrong side of the ship's skin, watching as Dag and Trina and Lane go bat-shit crazy trying all the things from all the manuals, guides, and computer simulations that they gave up their nights and ballgames and weekends to study (and then try a few hundred more things that aren't in those manuals), after you realize they can't think of anything else and you're still out here and you cut yourself loose to spare their feelings and you rotate slowly into space for hours, or days, or weeks while your suit drains its battery pack and you shut off the heads-up to save the last few minutes, only after all that work, and pain, and suffering, that you look with your oxygen-starved brain into a universe so deep with its stars and galaxies, with its novae and pulsars and other things you cannot even pretend to imagine, that you say to yourself, "My God, how beautiful you are."

Ron's Afterword

Yes, that's right.

This is a complete story in a single, 249-word sentence. In a cliché of all clichés, it came to me literally in the shower. I remember being so insanely worried I was going to lose it that I shut the shower down, went sopping wet out to our bedroom to grab a notepad, and jotted the bulk of it down right then and there.

I wrote it originally for a unique anthology that Matt Bennardo edited. I loved seeing it there. So much fun. And the fact that Lisa (the wife/copyeditor) loved it made it all that much better.

On a bit of a lark, I sent it to Trevor at *Analog*, simply because it was short and I know editors are always looking for something they can use to fill space. As a strong rule, *Analog* does not accept reprints, but he liked this well enough to break that rule.

Yay me!

And thank goodness I shut off the shower!

A Note at the End

You've come to the end of *1101 Digital Stories in an Analog World*. If you enjoyed these stories, a review placed at your favorite bookseller is a great and appreciated way to pass the word.

Thank you so much for reading!

ABOUT RON COLLINS

Ron Collins is a bestselling Science Fiction author who writes across the spectrum of contemporary and speculative fiction. His short fiction has received a Writers of the Future prize and a CompuServe HOMer Award. His short story "The White Game" was nominated for the Short Mystery Fiction Society's Derringer Award.

With his daughter, Brigid, he also edited *Face the Strange, An Anthology of Speculative Fiction.*

Follow Ron at:

Typosphere
.com

Join Ron's Reader List: http://typosphere.com/newsletter

Glamour of the God-Touched
(Book 1 of *Saga of the God-Touched Mage*)

STARCRUISE
(a short story in the *Stealing the Sun* universe)

Other Work by Ron Collins

<u>Novels</u>

Stealing the Sun (9 books)
Saga of the God-Touched Mage (8 books)
The PEBA Diaries (2 books)
The Knight Deception
Wakers

Fastballs and Fairies (3 Books), with Brigid Collins
Cruise Brothers Novels (3 Books), with Jeff Collins

<u>Collections</u>

1100 Digital Stories in an Analog World
They Came Back
Collins Creek (3 volumes)
Tomorrow in All the Worlds
Picasso's Cat & Other Stories
Five Magics
Seven Days in May, with John C. Bodin

<u>Poetry</u>

Five Seven Five

<u>Nonfiction</u>

On Writing (And Reading!) Short
On Creating (And Celebrating!) Characters

Acknowledgements

As with the companion volume to this one, I would like to thank the two editors, Stanley Schmidt and Trevor Quachri, as well as Emily Hockaday and every other member of the staff at *Analog Science Fiction and Fact* over the years. They have been and continue to be eminently professional and a joy to work with.

I would also like to thank *Analog* readers through those same years, especially those who have taken the time to send me notes of encouragement regarding one story or another, as they saw fit.

It is such a pleasure to see my work in this publication, and that would not have happened without their support.

I thank, also, Lisa—the true love of my life, and the greatest copyeditor and typo crusher who ever existed. She is the best of everything, really. I guarantee that *any* errors found in any of my work have been created after she got her hands on it.

Special Thanks

I need to take a moment to thank all the people who backed this project through Kickstarter. Without them, this volume would not exist.

Alan Langford
Alexander Hale
Andy F
Annie Reed
Anonymous Reader
António Matos
Antony Jordan
Arend van 't Oever
Bob Clemens
Bonnie Elizabeth
Brígid Chillers
C.A. Rowland
Céline Malgen
Christian Meyer
Craig Garvie
Daniele Caracchi
David H. Hendrickson
David Holzborn
David Perlmutter
David Sandilands
Dawn Blair
Dean Wesley Smith
Dwayne Plain
E.M. Middel
E.R. Paskey
Elizabeth W.
Eric Farmer
Giovanni Venturi
Greg Levick
Jim Gotaas

Joseph Procopio
Judy McClain
Kal Powell
Kat A
Kate MacLeod
Kate Scully
Lisa Silverthorne
Luis Manuel Sánchez García
maileguy
Margit Hofmann
Mark Newman
Mark Nuzzi
Mary Jo Rabe
Meyari McFarland
Michael A. Burstein
Michael Warren Lucas
Patrick Hay
Paul S.
Paul Walker
Rev. Slick Sellers
Richard O'Shea
Risa Scranton
Rowan Stone
Ruth Ann Orlansky
Ryan M. Williams
Stephen Michael Kellat
Two Renegade Appalachians
Ultra Bithalver
Victoria P